Coveting

Love & Revenge

A Perilously Pretty Novel

By

Haven Cage

This is a work of fiction. Any similarity between the characters and situations within its pages and places or persons, living or dead, is unintentional and coincidental.

All artwork, on the cover and within this publication, was created by Haven Cage. Stock images used in artwork were purchased from Depositphotos.com. The cover model is Olivia, and the photographer is Kathy Giannoulis. You can find Kathy on Instagram at https://www.instagram.com/kathygiannoulis/ and at Shutterstock at https://www.shutterstock.com/g/kathySG.

ISBN: 978-1-7330702-1-8

Published by Haven Cage, LLC

United States

To my son.

I would do anything for you.

In loving memory of the father who watched over me like I was his own, even though I wasn't.

Acknowledgments

Each passing year, I meet more and more amazing people in the book world that become faithful readers, but also, close friends. Thanks to all the avid book-lovers that make my world go 'round. You hold me high and give me the courage to keep writing.

To my wonderful beta readers, your loyalty to me and my work warms my heart every time you step up to read one of my books! Thank you for thinking I'm worth your time, ladies.

Dina Alexander, Tammy Becraft, LaChelle Funk, Cheryl Johnson, Janise Tedlock, and Diana Quiett

Thanks to my editor, Jaclyn Lee. I'm so lucky to have found you. I hope our writing relationship, and our friendship, continues for years to come. You expect a little more of me each time we do this dance, and it forces me to improve my craft. I appreciate your dedication to making me a better writer!

Thanks to my awesome family, friends, and co-workers. I'm blessed to have your continued support. So many writers don't receive the amazing support from their family and friends that you've given me. Love you!

Chapter One

~ August 24th, 1871 ~

Crack.

The iron's edge sunk into his head like an ax striking a ripe cantaloupe on a warm summer afternoon.

I gripped the icy metallic handle tighter, preparing to deliver another blow. Frozen in place, I watched anxiously for the man to accept what I did and keel over.

He spun on his heels drunkenly. The poor man's mouth dropped open, his brows angling up in stark confusion. His left pupil ballooned to the size of a nickel, black engulfing the toffee brown of his iris.

I covered my mouth with a shaky hand.

Mr. Kingly staggered backward. His eyes rolled to the back of his head, and he collapsed to the floor like a sack of grain.

Oh my God. What have I done?

He didn't warn me. Edison didn't tell me it would be so…messy. So…bloody.

Why did I do this?

Something warm and goopy trickled down my left index finger.

I wiped my hand on my skirt.

Instantly realizing my carelessness, I gaped down at the layers of silk covering my thigh. Fine cerulean threads absorbed the red handprint I smeared along the folds of fabric.

There it was, a single blemish of indisputable evidence forever marking my clothes. A scarlet testament to my wrongdoings.

The room set into a dizzying spin around me. I threw my hand against the wall, steadying myself. My breath quickened. The bones of my corset dug into my ribs.

I can't breathe. I'm going to faint right here…next to Mr. Kingly. They'll find me beside his dead body and know, without a doubt, it was me.

Slumping over, I tugged at the edge of my bodice, struggling to gulp down air.

Why didn't I just tell him no?

"You know why, Syn," I whispered between jagged breaths.

A soft gasp behind me broke the chaos of my shamed thoughts.

I twirled around, the hem of my bell-shaped dress dragging in the pool of blood collecting around my feet. The added weight of Mr. Kingly's life-force soaking into the lofty fabric weighted me down like fifty-pound shackles fastened to my ankles.

Tula stood at the foot of the cellar stairs quiet as a mouse, her glossy eyes fixed on me and her lips pressed into a thin line. She, somehow, sneaked up behind me.

A rock settled in my stomach. Had she seen me?

I wound my shoulder in a small circle, the clothing iron heavy in my right hand. Chilling and cumbersome like Mr. Kingly's blood, it taunted me with the crime I committed minutes before and pulled at my strained joint.

"I thought I told you to remain on the first floor during the party." I glanced down at her feet, and her bare toes curled sheepishly.

The clever girl removed her shoes so I wouldn't hear her coming.

She was always looking out for me, worrying Edison's demands would break me one day. I should have known she wouldn't keep her distance from me tonight. Tula was never far from me, ready to pick me up and give me strength whenever she suspected I was falling too deep into despair.

She picked at an ivory button on her sleeve, her emerald eyes glossy. She was particularly concerned about how I'd handle tonight.

The fifteen-year-old girl with mellow beige skin and a spray of dark-brown freckles bridging her cheeks and nose stared at me. Ignoring my remark about her tending to the gathering, she remained quiet and clung to her own inner strength. Most people would shriek and run if they walked in on a tableau such as this. Aside from a slight tremble in her shoulder, Tula maintained more self-control than I was capable of mustering at the moment.

She was the only staff left after Edison began gradually releasing the house help of their duties over the past months. He never told me his reasons for dispatching the caregivers, but he didn't have to. Being his governess, I wasn't entitled to any details he wasn't keen on sharing. Yet, when he took me to his bed, I was no longer the house help. I was the woman he promised to wed so many years ago. We were equals between the sheets—at least that's the way it was when our relationship began twelve years ago.

I should have known better. I should have seen our affair for what it was—a dumb, low-class girl helping her master forget the loss of his family.

Now, I'm a dumb, low-class murderer.

Tula's gaze swept over the bloodied body on the floor. The corners of her mouth turned down.

"Don't look at him," I snapped, sliding to my right to impede her view of Mr. Kingly's misshapen head.

My heart ached for her to see me in the midst of such violence. How would she view me now? Would she think me a monster?

She was my only friend on this god-forsaken plantation. Of all the staff we've had come in and out of our home, and our lives, over the past decade, Tula was indeed my favorite.

She was like a daughter to me.

Since Edison found her, hiding in our bushes at the young age of nine, we'd become quite attached to each other. The poor child was scared half to death when he scooped her up and carried her inside.

She refused to utter a single word for the first three days on our plantation, but I finally coaxed her into speaking. She followed me out to our garden one day, and I taught her about the foxglove growing there. Once I told her it was poisonous, her eyes lit up. She was amazed we kept dangerous plants on the property, and a flood of questions tumbled out of her tiny heart-shaped mouth. After that, we were inseparable.

She never told me what she was running from, and I felt so sorry for the child, so I didn't prod too much to find out. I assumed whatever drove the girl to Edison's homestead was too traumatic and painful for her to talk about. Yet, here I was, trying to guard her in one breath then bringing more trauma to her life the next.

There were days I wished she laid down to rest in someone else's yard. She might be happier…safer.

An onslaught of muffled music clambered to life above our heads, jolting my thoughts back to the cellar. The band of violins and horns was beginning the night's festivities, inviting our guests to dance. Men's boots and ladies' heels clacked along the hardwoods in predictable rhythm with the music, and I was reminded of the people awaiting my attendance.

I glared up at the floor beams, biting my bottom lip.

I still had a long night ahead. There was no time to wallow in pity and remorse. The minute I was done with Mr. Kingly, I was expected to put on a smile and serve the town's most important money-makers.

Tula's unruffled face turned up to the ceiling.

I took advantage of her distraction and drew the heavy iron toward the back of my thigh, hoping she might not notice it.

Her emerald-green eyes shot down to my hand, catching my motion. Her attention latched onto the very thing she used to press our linen each morning. Now, every time she looked at it, she'd see a weapon, a bludgeoning hunk of metal covered in a stranger's blood.

"It's okay, Tula." My words were thick in my throat like lumpy porridge. It wasn't okay. None of this was okay. My soul would burn in hell for what I did. The Devil was alive in our house, and I was at his mercy. I was a slave to his wickedness.

A trail of dust drifted from the cracks, knocked loose by the mongrels dancing on the first floor, and trickled to my nose. I wrinkled my face and blew at the dirt with a frustrated huff.

Frowning, I wished I hadn't woken up this morning. I should have pretended I was ill and stayed in bed. Perhaps, Edison wouldn't have made me entertain the high-society pigeons upstairs. Maybe, if I told him I had the flu, he would have postponed the party, and Mr. Kingly would be at home right now…alive.

Edison was such a humble and caring man when I met him, but he'd changed. He was an emotional landslide, beginning the day his family met their demise over a thirteen years ago, then snowballing as his greed grew in recent years.

Our relationship deteriorated.

He deteriorated.

"Ma'am, he's…he's still moving." Her frail hand shook, pointing to the blonde gentleman flattened on the floor.

Tula's soft warning dissipated my "what-ifs" like a fan wafting away a tendril of smoke. I twisted to see Mr. Kingly's body wriggle at my heels.

There was no use pondering the many scenarios that might have led to a different, more pleasant ending to this evening. Edison would have found a way to force me to this occasion, one way or another. Whether tonight or another night, I would have led Mr. Kingly to his doom.

My hands were tinted with his blood, my soul was tarnished with a crimson stain water would never wash away. Nothing could change that.

Mr. Kingly's lips moved lazily around silent pleas for help.

My heart sped like galloping horses. I couldn't leave him alive. Edison would concoct some way to punish me if I didn't finish his bidding, and he'd use Tula to do it.

He was an expert when it came to using the girl to get what he wanted from me.

Edison often saddled Tula with charming secrets out of his fellow businessmen, or spying on them, insisting they were out to get him in some way. In the case of poor Mr. Kingly, she was ordered to kill the gentleman who ventured too close to Edison's bottom-line. He guaranteed her compliance by promising her days of starvation, separation from me, or physical punishment should she refuse. Fear of hunger, loneliness, and pain would persuade anyone to do what was asked of them.

In the end, he made the threats, but he knew he wouldn't have to act on them. He knew I'd take on the damning burdens to save Tula from throwing away her innocence, and, also, to keep him from unleashing his wrath on her.

We dared to challenge him once. It only took one time for him to convince us he was a man of his word. He locked Tula in this very cellar. I searched everywhere for the key, but he'd hidden it too well. I kneeled on the dirty floor, crying, shoving morsels of bread and cheese through the sliver of opening under the door so she could have something to sustain her until he allowed her freedom.

Two days later, he opened the cellar, but only after I seduced secrets from a farmer Edison was acquainted with and relayed them to him.

He realized how easily I gave into his demands when it came to Tula's well-being, and manipulated me through her every time he deemed some horrid mission necessary.

I saw a glimpse of the real man Edison Pike was becoming that day.

I witnessed what he was capable of doing without remorse and wondered what else he might be willing to do for the sake of getting what he wanted.

He shoved a splinter of fear under my skin so deep I couldn't pick it out, no matter how hard I tried. He knew how to twist my maternal fondness for Tula and took full advantage of the knowledge any chance he got.

Unfortunately, I didn't have to wonder anymore. The man lying at my feet was a prime example of how far Edison would go.

Glancing back at Tula, I contemplated her fate if I didn't put an end to Mr. Kingly.

Edison's response to my pleas when I begged him to reconsider his request last night echoed against my skull.

"I don't care who does it, so long as it gets done, Synthia. It's either you kill the weasel or Tula kills him. I think you would rather do the job, though." He smirked.

I opened my lips to protest, but he cut me off.

"Go against my wishes, and I'll drag her behind a horse then bury her in a coffin, alive, for a week."

A pang of dread bloomed in my chest, large and full, like a peony. I shook my head and pinched the bridge of my nose.

Never mind Edison's dreaded punishment if I let Mr. Kingly live, Savannah's authorities would likely imprison me for life, or worse, if they found out I murdered this gentleman.

I might be able to escape the death penalty if I was crafty enough with my reasons. Perhaps, being a governess—a working woman with a respectable title—would afford me the least bit of sympathy. Tula, though, would surely swing in the courtyard. Being a simple maid of mixed heritage, she had no stature to help her defend such accusations.

"Ma'am?" Tula whispered, stepping forward. Her lower lip quivered, and a tear spilled along the ridge of her slightly up-turned nose. She reached out to take the iron form my grasp, but I jerked it away.

"You'll not muck up your hands with this, girl," I snarled, angry she'd even attempt to sully her good name.

I swiped a speck of cool wetness dripping down my cheek and studied the crimson blood. The crimson droplet soaked into the fine ridges of my skin, highlighting the heart and fate lines creasing my palm.

Would I ever get it clean? Would it stain the lines of my hands for years to come, incriminating me even further?

I turned toward Mr. Kingly, putting on some resemblance of calm composure like a dark cloak draped around my shoulders. "I'll handle this, Tula. Please, go upstairs and tend to the guests. I'll be up in a bit. Make sure the door to the kitchen is locked so they don't mosey in while I'm heading up the cook's stairs. Wouldn't want any nosey-bodies seeing me like this."

She stepped forward. "But, mistress—"

I raised a dismissive hand, insisting she do what I said without arguing.

Tula ascended the steps, the sound of her bare feet pounding against the stairs lightening towards the top. The door creaked shut behind her, and I bowed my head, thanking God she wasn't there to witness Mr. Kingly's ruination anymore.

A draft whistled through a crack in the cellar hatch leading to the back yard. I shivered, letting my mind stray from the task at hand for a minute longer.

The door was there. Edison wouldn't see me go. I could run. I could leave all this behind me as if it never happened.

The lantern's dim glow waved from the shelf along the back wall, flickering under the current of fresh air stirring the stuffy atmosphere.

I was only teasing myself. I couldn't leave this place. My efforts to evade him never worked out, and we always ended up right back in his clutches.

My gaze roamed, aimlessly, over the dusty bottles of wine lining the shelves next to the lantern. Stacks and stacks of the colored glass containers, filled to the brim with the best wine, surrounded me.

Edison imported the bottles directly from Italy, the highest quality he could afford with his meager fortune.

I scoffed at how selfish the man was. He spent a frivolous amount on the collection but refused to share it with our guests. Instead, they were served the cheapest wine he could find.

When I mentioned bringing a few bottles up for the gathering this morning, he whipped around in his desk chair and barked, "Absolutely not. All the socialites visiting for this party aren't worth a half cent as a whole. Why should I offer them such luxuries when they'll never know how to appreciate it like I do?"

Another breeze whistled in, compelling the lantern's light to dance across the glass cylinders happily, as if there wasn't a man dying only feet away. The soft glow shone through the bottles like a prism, casting a lovely kaleidoscope of green and rose over Mr. Kingly's head.

I shuttered, blinking away my last remnants of weakness to replace it with numb resolution.

Mr. Kingly groaned, sputtering on his own blood.

He was certainly worth more than a half cent. He was an up-and-coming businessman who recently moved to the area in search of a stronger footing in textiles.

I ventured to guess it was why my dear Edison wanted to kill him. If Mr. Kingly gained traction in the trade as he intended, he might have made Edison's lot in the Georgia indigo and cotton industry suffer, particularly his local holdings.

Stepping forward, I bent over the young, kind-looking man and peered into his frightened, hazy eyes. His skull was dented and seeping where I slammed the iron's edge minutes before. I bit into my cheek, allowing the sharp pain to keep the smidgeon of guilt from overpowering my numb emotions.

The unsuspecting man followed me into the cellar thinking I'd let him taste some of our private libations. He was already two sheets in the wind when I'd asked him to help me bring up a case for the party. As soon as he turned his back, I gulped down bile leaching up my throat and snatched the iron from the shelf.

I did not want to witness my own actions, so I squeezed my eyelids closed. Drawing my weapon wielding hand into the air, I held my breath and swung hard in his direction. I wanted to pretend it was someone else's hands cracking his head open with the hunk of metal, but I could not escape the truth of my actions when I felt his skull buckle under my attack.

Memorizing the deep lines of terror creasing his forehead and the slackness of Mr. Kingly's gaping jaw, I concluded the reality of killing him would constantly whisper to me from the back of my mind. I would have nightmares about it for the rest of my days.

An image of Tula's slender body, broken and dirty, dragging behind Edison's snow-white steed flashed through my mind. That vision was quickly replaced by a flash of her neck snapping at an unnatural angle as she hung by a rope in the courtyard. Freezing fingers of foreboding dismay wrapped their way around my bones and clawed at my soul.

I bent down to look into Mr. Kingly's good eye, his own fear reflecting at me. "I'm so sorry, sir. Please know I didn't have any other choice. I had to save her from this misery," I beseeched him. "Now, I'm going to save you from yours."

Gripping both hands around the heavy iron, I lugged it over my head and swung until Mr. Kingly was no more.

Chapter Two

I ran up the cook's stairwell as fast as my bulky dress would allow. My bloodied fists fisted tighter around the layers of heavy skirts and crinoline, hefting it up to give my feet a better chance of making the next step without fail.

I choked back sobs of regret, clamping my teeth together to barricade my emotions.

I stumbled on the last step, banging my shoulder into the wall. A yelp of despair escaped my lips, but I quickly cinched them shut, denying the full-on wails I longed to unleash.

Leaning into the hard surface with my eyes closed, I settled my erratic breaths. The sweet, high notes of a violin floated from the ballroom, reverberating off the lustrous mint and gold-embellished wallpaper. The sound vibrated against my shoulder, soothing the angst tightening my muscles.

I pictured bluebloods dancing in synchronized steps above Mr. Kingly's corpse without any notions of what transpired mere feet below their pretentious heels. The sooner I catered to them, the sooner I could get them out of the house. The idea urged me up the last step.

I turned the corner, entering the long hallway stretching along the rear of the house. It was dark, save for the setting sun shining through a circle of stained glass at the end of the hall. A chute of pink light extended from the elegant depiction of a rose in the window down to the indigo rug at the foot of my bedroom door, marking my destination.

I burst through the entrance, slammed the door closed, then slumped against the wood slab blocking me from the rest of the world.

Heaving loud breaths, I wrestled against the confines of my clothes to find air. Tears poured down my cheeks. The room felt hot, stale…sticky from my iniquities and the humid, southern heat.

Reaching behind my neck, I worked to get my dress undone. My fingers fumbled with the small buttons. "Get off," I whispered. "Get off, get off," I repeated, growing louder and more frantic each time. I tore at the tiny silk pearls lining the back of my bodice, determined to break free.

Usually, Tula assisted me in dressing and undressing, but I didn't care what damage I caused the threads. I'd enjoy giving it back to Edison in a heap of blood-stained rags.

The first button popped loose, then the second, giving me enough room to wiggle my shoulders and arms out through the neckline. I shoved the gold-embroidered top down to my waist.

Plucking the hooks out of each loop, I unfastened the top portion of my corset. My bosom spilled forth, relieving the constant compression around my lungs. I drew in the deepest, most lung-filling, breath I'd taken since donning the garment earlier this morning.

I wrapped my hand around the carved post at the foot of my bed, steadying my weak posture. Hunching over, I closed my eyes.

Mr. Kingly's blonde curls, sopping with red, flashed against the backs of my eyelids. I gagged, recalling how his forehead split open, peeling back from his skull like the outer petals of a rose curling away from its center bloom. The arch of his left brow was flattened, the flesh there fileted into jagged shreds of meat crinkling back from his shattered bones.

I doubled over, vomit flooding my mouth. The remnants of my stomach breached my lips and splattered all over my cerulean skirt.

The door flung open behind me, cracking against my armoire.

I jumped and spun around, covering my chest with my forearms.

Edison strolled into the room, leaving the door wide open. His deep brown eyes wandered over my bare flesh hungrily before scrutinizing the state of my dress. His nostrils flared, and his handsome features wrinkled with disgust.

"I'm assuming it's done?" He stepped closer, clasping his hands at the base of his back.

I nodded but refused to admit it vocally.

"The body?" Edison paused at my side, eyeing the curves of my breasts.

"You can take care of it yourself," I gritted, notching my chin higher to hide how spineless I felt near him.

His eyes shot up to meet mine, locking me in his scornful stare. He grinned then licked his thin lips. Returning his gaze to my bosom, he lifted a hand and traced the soft globes of flesh pinned beneath my arms.

I straightened my back, staring into his mahogany eyes, making it clear I would not cower under his touch. I might have to do what he says to avoid his wrath on me and Tula, but I would not do it with an ounce of fear on my face.

Noting the defiant shift in my posture, Edison ran his tongue across his teeth then pursed his lips. His demanding hand nudged my arms aside, giving him full access to my body. Rough fingers brushed over my peaked nipples, tightening the dusky rose tips into aching points.

Pressing my lips together, I swallowed back the moan of pleasure he was eliciting. I wouldn't give him the satisfaction. I closed my eyes and focused on keeping my strength while his feather-light caresses turned into vulgar groping.

There was a time when I cared for Edison. A time I admired the man I was betrothed to. I was proud to call him my lover just months ago. He was intelligent, striking, and used to be kind. Something changed when his business climbed to new heights, securing his stature in a new class of peers. He morphed into a money-hungry tyrant and never looked back.

I supposed there was some part of me that still loved him. It was apparent in the way my body reacted to his touch.

We'd spent years together. In the beginning, Edison hired me to take care of his loving wife and two small children. I'd considered looking after his wonderful family a blessing. Steady work in the Pike house was exactly what I needed to leave my fruitless family thousands of miles behind.

The only thing I had left to offer a man willing to consider me for marriage was the prestige of my name. Being in my late twenties then, I was older than most women desired for matrimony. Unfortunately, the James' legacy was fading quicker than the money my parents squandered away, and my name wasn't as enticing as it once was.

There was nothing in my future if I remained in Oregon. Edison made me an offer while visiting my town on a business trip. He wanted me to be his governess. I was thrilled at the prospect of a new life and accepted without hesitation. Weeks later, I moved to Savannah, Georgia, leaving everything I knew behind.

Shortly after my relocation, Mrs. Pike and her children perished in a house fire. It was a day that weighed heavy on both our shoulders. Edison was away on a business trip, and I was in town at the market. Neither of us were there to save them.

Since I'd grown close to the children and my mistress, my own feelings of guilt and loss rivaled Edison's. Through the pain, we found comfort in one another.

Our relationship flourished on our shared sadness. We promised each other love and loyalty. He promised to marry me.

We endured the trials of discovering I'm barren, battled the doubtful opinions of locals who insisted he'd never get his business running, and nurtured our crops from seeds to something profitable in the harsh Southern economy.

I was there, with him, through it all. It's hard to discount so much history with a person, but that was then.

Here we are now. A powerful man determined to have it all, and the forgotten lover of thirty-two swept up in his deceit, reduced to little more than a maid and murderess.

Warm, wine-sweetened breath blew across my ear. "Get yourself cleaned up, rosebud. Tula needs help with the guests, and I can't have you looking like filth." Edison released my tender breast and turned to leave. "I'll send the girl up," he called over his shoulder. "You can get rid of the body later."

My stomach sank. I gaped at him, staring at his broad back in disbelief. He was going to leave the clean-up to me as well. What was I supposed to do with a corpse?

Bitter acid crept up my throat, and I swallowed hard. I'd have to see Mr. Kingly again, see the way I beat his head until it crumbled like the hard shell of a nut, his brain laying out for all to observe. I'd have to revisit the terrible thing I did before I even had a chance to adjust to the arduous chains of guilt winding around my heart.

I hurried toward the door, slamming it shut. Tears poured down my cheeks. I slid to the floor, clenching fistfuls of my dress until my knuckles turned white.

I released the sob I'd held for so long. Curling down to my knees, ignore the world for a little bit longer and allowed myself the outburst I deserved.

Chapter Three

"Who's down there?" I asked Tula, sliding my arms into the clean shift she held out for me.

She looped the gauzy fabric over my head. "Everyone ma'am. Those important in the thread business, anyway.

"Mr. Riley and Miss Williams seem to be gettin' on nicely. I bet if he keeps givin' her guff 'bout not being able to get a date for the ball, she'll take pity on him and let the deprived man in her drawers before the night's up."

I gasped, tugging my undergarment down from my face so I could glower at her properly. "Tula," I scolded, hiding my mild amusement.

She was too direct for her own good most days, but what she said about Mr. Riley was true. He *was* hard up for finding a mistress as of late. Seems he'd tell the single ladies anything to get a modicum of attention after his dear Ms. Gray decided against his offer to marry.

"You shouldn't make such assumptions about what our guests do behind closed doors. It's not your business to tend to. Besides," I said, snatching the corset she'd retrieved from the bed, "I give Miss Williams more credit than that. Surely, she'd make him wait until calling on her at least three times." Grinning, I gave her a mischievous side glance.

Tula's eyes widened, and she threw a hand over her mouth to stifle a giggle.

I winked, my own giggle bubbling to the surface. Resuming my work, I fastened each small hook on my corset then turned away from the girl, motioning for her to tighten my laces.

Tula pulled the ribbons taut. My breath shortened, and I almost welcomed the constrained feeling I cursed earlier in the evening. It gave me a sense of control again. Bound by the everyday piece of clothing, I slipped into the person I was supposed to be amidst public eyes. I was Mr. Pike's governess, not his shameful murderer.

Once Tula finished with my laces, she gathered my corset cover, cage, and petticoats, and helped me settle those into place.

She flopped down on my bed, dragging my soiled dress onto her lap. Her fingers rubbed over the blood drying on the hem, and she frowned. Glancing up under her long black lashes, she asked, "You'll be alright, Ms. James?"

I hesitated, my gaze drifting over the blood-stained edge of my only other evening gown. I didn't know if I would be okay in all this. My fate hurled me into a deep, dark well, and I was still falling. I couldn't be sure what awaited me at the bottom, but it surely wouldn't be a pleasant landing.

I pressed my lips together and nodded, reassuring the girl as best as I could. "It's time to get down there. We can't hide forever. Help me finish?" I asked, reaching for my fresh dress.

She stood and gathered the heavy skirt into a bunched loop for me to shimmy into. "I'll do what I can to get the sin outta your dress."

Straightening my sleeves, I nodded appreciatively. "We'll work on it in the morning. It's likely I'll have more garments covered in blood before the nights done."

Tula stilled. "The body? You have to hide it too?"

Pinning back the dark curl dangling on my cheek, I met her gaze and gave a somber, half-hearted smile. "I just don't understand the man anymore. He's…he's not the kind gentleman I came to work for and fell in love with. I've never seen such greed in a soul's eyes before."

Her hands angrily fastened the buttons along my spine. "Ain't right. He's usin' you, Ms. James. Must be somethin' we can do to get outta this. Can't we just run away?" She spun me around, her face alight with hope. "I'll leave with you tonight. We can keep goin' 'til we reach the western ocean you told me 'bout. We can take care of each other, Ms. James."

I closed my hands around hers and pulled them against my heart. "I'd gladly show you the world, child, but I have no means to keep either of us afloat on our own. We'd starve or end up fallen women on the streets, selling any dignity we have." Releasing her hands, I cupped her cheeks and kissed her forehead. "I just can't walk you into a life like that. Besides, we've tried to leave before, and he always finds us, Tula." I patted her cheeks. "We'll find a way around this soon, I promise, sweet girl."

Her shoulders fell. A tear rolled down her cheek. "Best we join 'em then. Mary will need to go home soon. The Murrays' only lent her help until midnight."

I nodded, clasping her fingers with mine.

We left my room in silence, mentally preparing for the masquerade we would have to uphold for the rest of the evening. The dim hallway leading to the cook's staircase was just long enough for me to assemble some sort of normal, unraveled disposition.

I squeezed Tula's hand once, giving her a reassuring smile, then descended the stairs at the end of the corridor ahead of her.

Stepping into the kitchen, I flicked my hand toward the pantry without a word. I didn't have to give Tula verbal directions anymore. She was accustomed to our hosting routine and knew exactly what foods Edison expected us to serve.

Obeying my gesture, she hurried into the dark doorway to retrieve the necessary goods.

I swiped my sweaty palms down the front of my dress and inhaled a cleansing breath. Evaluating the cakes and cookies Tula and Mary set out, I pushed the earlier events from my mind.

"Bring me the bread and jam while you're in there," I called over my shoulder. Swaying back and forth at the kitchen counter, I quickly arranged cheese chunks and bunches of muscadines on freshly polished silver trays. Small lace doilies draped the trays, creating an elegant, yet simple, presentation for the party attendees.

Details were important to Edison. Always put on a good show, make them believe you are high society, even if you are not.

The kitchen door swung open. My gaze darted up to youthful round face poking around the edge.

Mary sniffled, her thin brows pushed up in concern. "Mr. Pike is growin' impatient. I tol' 'im Tula went up after you, but he doesn't seem pleased, Ms. James," she explained with an Irish cadence. Her perpetual rosy cheeks plumped around a puff of air and she blew out in aggravation. "The blasted man sent me in here to check on you. Is there somtin' else I should be doin' to help?"

I shook my head, traces of an amused smile pulling at the corners of my mouth. "No, Mary. Keep circulating the beverages. Tula and I will be out soon." She was a rather frazzled girl most days, but I considered her delightful.

Mary disappeared behind the door, leaving it swinging in her wake.

Tula dashed through the pantry door, cradling a baguette, a glass jar, and four wine flutes against her chest.

"Hurry now," I encouraged, waving her to my side, "Mary's already rushed in here once, complaining Mr. Pike was looking for us."

She shifted her hand, securing the strawberry jam slipping from the crook of her elbow. "He can look for us all he wants, Ms. Unless he's gonna come in here and get the food ready himself, he's just gonna have ta wait 'til we're good and ready."

Rolling my eyes at her, I unloaded the items from her arms and set them on the counter. "Tear the bread in pieces, put a dab of jam on each one, then bring the tray out," I instructed, pointing to the silver platter in front of her. I added the glasses to my tray and lifted it, carefully balancing it on my palm. "I'm going to go ahead, so he doesn't hunt us down."

If Edison hadn't let the other staff go, we wouldn't be rushed catering to his guests. Of course, if I didn't have to kill a man for him, he'd have his damned h'orderves already served too.

Shoving the door open with my hip, I drew in a breath and fixed a warm, deceiving smile on my face.

I approached those closest to me, mindful not to interrupt their conversations, and made my way around the room. Eighteen people later, I found myself edging closer to Edison. Our glances met, but our expressions remained unaffected by each other's presence.

Once upon a time, my cheeks flushed and heart raced anytime he looked at me. The way his mouth twitched adorably, hiding a rogue smile, set my veins on fire with need once upon a time. Now, we regarded one another with dangerous uncertainty and fake pleasantries, his twitching a mark of the dark secrets he guarded.

What did we become?

"Synthia," Edison greeted in a domineering tone.

I approached him with the serving tray, bobbing in a small, polite curtsy. My fingers clenched the silver tight while visions of smacking him in his smug face with the flat pan flourished in my mind.

"Mr. and Mrs. Quinn, this is my governess, Ms. Synthia James," Edison introduced. This was the way it always was at these gatherings; I was downgraded to his help, nothing more.

I smiled warmly, holding the tray out to them. "Good evening. Would you care for some cheese?"

"Well now, that's a nice little spread you have there," Mr. Quinn said, removing his hand from his robust belly to reach for a chunk of goat cheese.

Mrs. Quinn chortled. "I wasn't aware you had children, Mr. Pike. I would love to meet them. Are they with their mother?" Her curious eyes wandered over the guests, searching for reasons why a man such as Edison might keep a governess.

A shadow of repressed grief darkened his chestnut eyes. Lucky for him, I was the only one who recognized it. No one else knew what it was like to see the man so laden with sadness, he curled into a ball and cried like a baby.

He dipped his head and forced a smile to curl his lips. "Yes, my sweet Diane took them to her mother's."

The lie slipped off his tongue with the ease of truth. He'd said it so many times before, always feeling the need to fend off his meddlesome business partners. Edison was convinced it made him more respectable to be a family man, rather than a widower keeping a mistress.

His warning gaze landed on me. I kept his lie, lowering my eyes to the half-empty cheese tray.

"Ah, there he is," Mr. Quinn gushed loudly, waving to an arriving guest in the foyer. "Come, sir. Meet our strapping host."

The gentleman moved through the room with a confidence that made his broad shoulders appear wider and his lengthy frame taller. He held out a hand, greeting Mr. Quinn with a smile and a shake. He turned to Mrs. Quinn and took off his shiny black top hat. "Madam."

His regal features, and the civilized manner in which he presented himself, implied money and class; yet, tipping my head the tiniest notch to the side, I noticed a sheen of sun-kissed highlights in his auburn hair, like he spent his days outdoors, working under the sun.

He gently took Mrs. Quinn's fingers in his and bent to kiss the back of her hand. My eyes homed in on hints of dirt blackening his cuticles. He was a man who knew manual labor.

The substantially older woman giggled coyly, a blush spreading from her sagging neck to her heavily powdered cheeks. "Oh dear, why so formal?" Mrs. Quinn flapped her green silk fan in front of her face rapidly. "We're all friends here, right?" She sidled into the gentleman's side, batting her thin eyelashes relentlessly.

Her husband snatched a fresh wine flute from young Mary's tray. Mr. Quinn was too busy devilishly eyeing the help to notice Mrs. Quinn's flirting.

"Yes, yes, we're all men of power here, Mr. Burke. No need to act shy around us," Mr. Quinn prattled, his gaze lingering on the back of Mary's skirt until she was out of view. "This is Silas Burke," he waggled his chunky fingers distractedly at the new guest. "And, this, Silas, is Edison Pike. The gentleman I told you about."

Mr. Quinn gulped down a large swallow of his cheap wine. He rested his beefy hand back on his profound belly and afforded my body a hungry glance from toe to head before returning his focus to the men he introduced.

I bit my lip to refrain from scolding the impish old man's wandering attention and turned to leave.

Edison gripped my forearm, jerking me to a stop.

I glared at his hand, tensing to jerk away from his grip, but thought better of making a scene.

Embarrassed, I scanned the guests crowded around us. Mr. Burke was the only one paying any heed. His gray eyes darted to Edison's fingers digging into my skin. His head tipped to the side, seeming to question Edison's rough action.

Could he see through the mask my employer wore? Was it possible Mr. Burke sensed Edison's controlling demeanor from one harsh grip on my arm and disapproved?

Edison smirked, locking gazes with Mr. Burke. He released my forearm and plucked a muscadine from the bunch I carried. Tossing it into his mouth, he gnashed his teeth into the fruit so hard, the muscles in his jaw clenched.

I lifted my tray toward Mr. Burke and smiled, trying to calm the swelling tension between the two men. "Would you like some cheese, sir? It's from our best goat. And I picked the muscadines myself. They flourish in our woods."

His kind eyes narrowed curiously. Mr. Burke picked up the hunk of cheese closest to the edge of the tray. His hand brushed my fingers in the process, sending a jolt of tingles up my arm.

My breath hitched. His callused skin sparked my senses to life, eliciting emotions long forgotten, emotions I once felt for Edison in those initial moments of our blooming love.

Mr. Burke's gaze remained on me while he bit into his cheese and chewed slowly. "Delicious," he murmured, the heat of desire flushing his golden skin with a hint of rose.

Everyone in the room vanished. No one existed except for me and Mr. Burke. I heard only the teasing inflection in his deep voice, his uneven breaths. The yearning gleam in his wise eyes matched my own unexpected bloom of need.

Edison cleared his throat.

I plunged back into the room filled with lively party attendants.

Resentment for Edison crept back into my gut, yanking me down from the cloud I was floating on.

"So, Silas, where are you from? I haven't heard your name around this part of town," Edison prodded.

Mr. Burke lifted a glass of wine from my tray and swigged the contents in one gulp. He set the empty flute back on my tray, his eyes lingering on me while answering Edison. "Oh, I've traveled a lot over the past year. Trying to figure out where I'd like to dig in my roots."

"Yes, Silas explored all the states. He's quite the wandering soul," Mrs. Quinn added. "He's bought the farm right behind yours, though, Edison. You two are neighbors now. Should make for an interesting partnership in the future. With his cotton crops and your indigo, you two could dominate the textile business." She lightly patted her hair, making sure every silver strand was still in the tight twist at the back of her head.

I tucked the rim of my tray against my stomach and lowered my eyes to the floor. It occurred to me how close Mr. Burke would be every day, and my heart fluttered.

"Is that right?" Edison asked with an undertone of aggravation. "I didn't realize the plot was for sale."

Mr. Burke raised his chin, grinning. "My mother is a cousin of old man Jenkins. He knew I was looking for something in the area and offered it to me at a fair price."

"I see."

From the corner of my eye, I saw Edison's fist tighten against his thigh.

He tried to wear Mr. Jenkins down for years, hoping to get the old coot's section of land. It had a great water supply and nestled up to the rear of Edison's land. Cotton grew abundantly there because of its sandy soil.

Edison's intentions were to buy the lot and do exactly what Mrs. Quinn suggested, but by himself. If he could own the highest producing cotton crops in the area, along with his very successful indigo plantation, Edison would certainly be one of the most powerful men in Savannah's textile industry.

Now, his chance was a bit farther out of reach.

A smirk tugged at the corner of my mouth, but I fought the urge to relish the thorn in Edison's side, afraid he would see it.

"So, what are your plans now?" Edison swallowed a bitter mouthful of his wine.

"Well…I've hired some farm-hands and their families who have experience raising cotton. I plan on learning everything I can from them and making a fruitful harvest by next fall."

Edison raised an inquisitive brow. "And your connections?"

Mr. Quinn slapped Edison on his back and chuckled. "That's why I invited him, son. I thought this would be the perfect opportunity for you two to meet and devise a plan which could bring us all fortune."

"Perhaps." Edison pursed his lips, eyeing Mr. Burke, a cloud of doubt and irritation swirling behind his quiet façade.

Mr. Burke dipped his head. "Perhaps," he agreed.

Mr. Quinn stretched up to whisper something in Edison's ear, distracting him from his new enemy. The moment Edison turned his head, Mr. Burke's gaze descended on me like a bear on a beehive. He devoured me with his eyes, like I was honey on a comb.

Heat rushed in my veins, flushing my cheeks. I couldn't decipher what Mr. Quinn and Edison discussed, but I didn't care. My mind was compelled by Mr. Burke leisurely, ravenously, perusing my body.

Mrs. Quinn nestled into Mr. Burke's side, her gloved hand softly petting his forearm. "What other states have you seen, Silas? I've only traveled the Southeast."

When Mr. Burke glanced at the old lady, his spell on me dissipated, finally letting me think clearly again. I turned my back to his hypnotizing eyes and tapped Edison on the shoulder.

Edison crooked his brow at me, motioning for Mr. Quinn to pause his secret conversation.

"Mary is due home soon. I'm going to see to the other guests once more before she goes."

He nodded, waving me away.

I made one more swift turn about the room, eager to put distance between me and our new neighbor. Considering how easily I forgot my wits around the man, I decided it was best to never speak or talk to him again.

I approached the next group of guests, huddled around the violinist, and dared a side-glance in Mr. Burke's direction.

One more look couldn't hurt, right?

Mr. Burke sat, alone, on Edison's royal blue settee across the room, one long leg propped on the other at his ankle. He lifted a half-full wine flute to his lips, watching me as if I was the only worthy entertainment in the room. His hand stilled a breath from his mouth when he realized I was looking back at him. A pleased grin formed behind the glass, and a deep, sinful dimple indented his cheek.

My knees became pudding. I inhaled deeply, trying to catch the air he'd stolen from me. The fire I felt when Edison looked at me in that way was a candle flame compared to the inferno raging in my core with Mr. Burke's attention on me.

"My dear, are you okay?"

I shook my head, rattling my thoughts back into order. A small woman in an ivory dress, layered with pretentious ruffles, rested her white glove on my shoulder. I recognized Ms. Lang as the wife of Mr. Claude Lang, owner of Savannah's bank. She was always pleasant to me, but her husband was an ogre.

She smiled sweetly. "Everything alright, darlin'?"

I returned her polite smile. "Yes…yes, I'm fine."

Ms. Lang dropped her hand from my arm and pushed her empty glass toward me. "I asked if you had any water, but you didn't answer. I thought you went mute all of a sudden." She giggled around a hiccup.

"I'll get you some, Ms. Lang. Be right back." I took her cup, happy to excuse myself from the ballroom.

One step into the kitchen, and I could breathe again. Mr. Burke turned me into a complete idiot. I needed to force myself to forget about the tall, alluring man with engaging eyes.

I poured well-water from an ewer into the empty cup and sat it on the counter. Doubling over, I braced myself on my palms and steeled myself against the needling memories of my crime…against the consuming thoughts of Mr. Burke.

"You can do this," I whispered. "Go out there and pretend there's not a dead body in the cellar. Pretend Mr. Burke never entered the house."

Gripping Ms. Lang's water, I relaxed my shoulders and ventured back into the den of beasts.

Though I didn't catch him spying on me again, the tingle of his eyes zapped through my body as I moved from one intoxicated visitor to another.

Morning crept closer. Exhausted guests, sobering from a long night of drinks and mingling, called for their carriages. With each person who cleared the room, I slowed my pace a little more, prolonging my next chore as long as possible—discarding Mr. Kingly's corpse.

I collected Mrs. Barrons' cloak and helped her secure it around her shoulders, fighting her fumbling fingers at the button. She'd be lucky to stay seated inside her open wagon tonight with all the tottering she was doing. God help her, if she falls out in an inebriated heap to land in a pile of horse shit.

I ushered Mrs. Barrons to the driver, holding onto her elbow to steer her in a straight line. "Please make sure she sits in the middle of the bench, sir."

"Yes, ma'am." The coachman took Mrs. Barrons' hand and braced her upper arm, guiding her up the carriage steps. She dipped to the right, nearly toppling on her ass. The wiry man made a hasty recovery, throwing his arm around her plump waist.

Mrs. Barrons gasped. She beamed at the coachman with wide eyes for a second then tipped her head back and unleashed a hearty laugh.

His swift hand shot out, snatching her feathery hat before it fell from her lop-sided hair. Once he finished loading Mrs. Barrons into the carriage, he grumbled something under his breath and claimed his own seat.

I shook my head from the front door, stifling a laugh.

Turning to verify all the guests were gone, I spotted Tula standing in a shadow down the hall. Her shoulders were slumped, and, even in the dim light, I could see she was ghostly pale.

I rushed to her, praying Edison hadn't said something to upset her. He often lashed out at her when he was in a dark mood. Since Mr. Burke showed up, his mood was anything but sunshine.

Stooping to eye-level with Tula, I wiped a tear rolling down her ashen cheek. "What is it, girl? What has you so frazzled?"

She sniveled, swiping her forearm across her snotty nose. "He," she hiccupped, "he gave me a new task."

I straightened, searching her face for more explanation. "And? What is he having you do that has you standing in the shadows crying?"

Just then, I heard the deep timber of Mr. Burke's voice nearing the front door. Edison came into view, leading him to the exit, talking about visiting Mr. Burke's estate soon.

"Mr. Pike ordered me to take care of him," Tula whispered.

"What? Take care of whom?" The moment the question left my lips, I knew the answer. Acid burned in my gut, along with the awful notion Edison's jealousy got the best of him tonight.

My eyes trailed to the two fetching men framed by the large mahogany door.

One, I loved vehemently in the past, but now, my feelings for him were little more than an occasional wave of hate-filled lust and disappointment at the monster he'd become. The other, I had no right to be attracted to. I was with Edison. We were entwined around each other like suffocating vines, a plethora of thorns needling into every tender part of our existence. There was too much history. Too many secrets. But the heat in Mr. Burke's gaze, and the subtle flare of my heart when we were close, made me yearn to flee the dismal life I was living—no matter what cost.

"Mr. Pike wants me to kill Mr. Burke," Tula whispered.

Chapter Four

"Why do you insist on involving her in your dirty deeds? Just leave Tula out of this." I gritted, hefting Mr. Kingly's legs up the cellar's back steps leading outside.

"Because I know how much she means to you. She's the only way I can get you to listen to reason," Edison grunted. He clenched Mr. Kingly's shoulders at his waist and followed me up the stairs.

"Reason?" I shrieked. "What reason? There is no good logic behind what you are doing…what you are making me do."

We lumbered out of the doorway, stumbling into the damp night with a sheet-wrapped corpse in our arms. Panting, Edison lifted Mr. Kingly's trunk enough to hoist him over the side of a small hay wagon in the back yard. I bent his stiff legs toward his chest so they wouldn't drag when I carried him to his final resting place.

I was the lucky one who got to haul the man into the woods, pulling the damn cart like an ox.

Edison raked back his long, sweat-slicked hair. Blood on his fingers left tinges of red in his black locks. He shook his head and closed his eyes. "You don't understand, rosebud. I'm doing this for us. I'm trying to eliminate the obstacles keeping us from our dreams." His eyelids popped open. He scanned over the large, aged manor we lived in and the unmaintained land around it. "We could have so much more than this."

Waving his hand, he gestured to the acres of indigo plants lit by the low-hanging yellow moon. "I've finally gotten the crops to flourish. I've partnered with the right men. Now, we just have to hold our position until our profits multiply. We are headed in the right direction, Synthia, but I can't have these outsiders coming in and staking claim on everything we've worked so hard to attain. They'll just piss on us and take all we have without a second thought."

I turned away from him, sickened by the road to success he mapped out. Gripping the neckline of my bodice, I pulled for an inch of freedom from its restraints. "Those are *your* dreams, Edison. If you want that type of success—drenched in the blood of innocent men—then you should be the one to shoulder the sin. I'm not your assassin, dammit."

I clamped my other hand around the side of the wagon. The splintered wood pierced my skin. I squeezed tighter, inciting more pain—anything to keep me from lashing out at him. Lord knew what would happen to Tula if I acted out of turn.

Edison stamped forward, wrapping his thick fingers around my upper arm. He jerked me around to face him. His teeth clamped together, and his lips drew into a sharp sneer. A glimpse of unbridled rage flashed over his stern features as he studied the barrage of emotions storming behind my eyes.

"You are mine, Syn. You'll be whatever I need you to be," he groaned, lowering his mouth to my neck.

Sharp teeth bit into my earlobe, zapping a hot beam of pleasure-pain to my core. I muted the moan rising in my throat but melted into his chest, a slave to my body's needs. Edison kissed below my ear, creating a path of wet, hot nips and licks to my collarbone. His tongue traced along the delicate bone, and I shuttered, a shiver of pleasure skittering up my spine.

Damn my body for betraying me, for making me reminisce about the love we once shared, for making me forget the corruption he'd embedded in our relationship.

I squeaked out a meek moan, and his head jerked up to look at me. I was a panting, wanton mess. Our mouths crashed together as if there wasn't a stitch of anger and resentment between us. Our lips and tongues took from each other. A hurricane of devastating turmoil and lust shadowed all sensibility advising us to think better of engaging one another.

He stopped abruptly, spinning me around in a whirlwind of clouded emotions. His large hand flattened between my shoulder blades, forcing me to bend over the edge of the wagon. I huffed out a surprised breath, but it didn't slow his frantic movements in the least.

He wrestled with my skirts, bunching them over my lower back. Stubby nails racked up the back of my thighs. I flinched, pressing into the wagon harder, and hissed from the stinging streaks he left on my skin. He dragged his fingers along my stockings and drawers until he found my waist-tie. In one lightning quick tug, my strings were undone, and Edison shoved my drawers down to my ankles.

My bare, wet flesh was suddenly exposed to the night air and his greedy hands. Fire blazed in my core. I didn't want this, yet I did. Echoes of our love resonated in my heart, but I hated this man.

His fingers slipped across my sex, finding me slick and quivering. I gasped. I was enthralled by the intense pleasure blazing under his touch.

He pressed his hand to my back and urged me to bend deeper. I obeyed, too overcome with need to refuse. He expelled a dark, throaty grunt and burrowed into my depths, stealing the breath from my lungs.

My eyes landed on Mr. Kingly's still form in the bed of the wagon. What kind of a person was I to let a man take me next to a corpse?

I pinched my eyelids shut and inhaled, sensing Edison's preparation to dominate my body.

He slid out of me then thrust back in, setting into a vigorous rhythm. He rocked me into the side of the wagon, again and again, until we both reached a quick, violent release minutes later.

It was one thing that never changed with us. No matter how much aversion we held for each other, our bodies always joined in pleasure without protest. Our past love fueled our insatiable drives before; now, our mutual anguish kept the coals smoldering.

Edison pulled out, panting behind me.

I straightened, hiking my undergarments back into place before letting the hem of my skirts fall to the dirt. Regret swooped in on my hazy thoughts, but it was too late. I couldn't change my impulsive lust for Edison any more than I could undo Kingly's death.

He tucked himself into his pants and fingered back the inky locks of hair dangling in his face. Instead of looking upon me with appreciation and love, his eyes lowered to the ground. "You should get him taken care of before the sun starts to rise."

Just like that, the false connection we had fell away, and I was his man-killing mistress again. His secret lady of the night.

Chapter Five

The wagon wheel tottered into a pie-sized hole halfway through the pasture, jerking me to a hard stop. My hands slid from the wooden handles, and a splinter threaded under the pad of my right index finger.

"Balls," I hissed, sucking on the tiny wound to stanch the bleeding. I sagged between the handles, leaning against the wagon's bed, and stared up at the sky. The stars shone bright tonight, dotting the endless blanket of darkness farther than I could see. The moon—a round, glowing orb of buttery yellow—hung so low, it nearly rested on the black treetops.

Owls screeched at one another from my shadowed destination ahead. Only twenty more yards or so, and I'd be able to escape the damning light of the moon. I could hide beneath the thick canopies of towering oaks and their veils of Spanish moss.

Slumping my shoulders, I glanced behind me at the sheet-cocooned body and sighed. "Oh, dear Mr. Kingly, if only you'd stayed home tonight."

A twig snapped in the distance. I jolted up from my perch, squinting at the tree line. Tilting my ear toward the sound, I waited, listening for another sign of movement. Nothing.

I was a lame duck, sitting here in the middle of a field under the light of the moon with the Almighty and any passing man to see.

I shoved the fly-away strands of hair from my face. Grabbing the handles, I gritted my teeth and rocked the burdensome wagon to and fro until it rolled out of the hole.

Mr. Kingly and I advanced, trudging through the waist-high grass. I widened my eyes, searching for the familiar pitch-black opening amidst the dark forest. It was the only spot wide enough to get the wagon through. I took ten steps closer, and my sights landed on the break in trees framed by low hanging branches.

I huffed out an exhausted breath, veering toward the entry I used often during the witching hours. It was my hiding spot to escape Edison and his control.

Ducking into the opening, I yanked the wagon in behind me. Fallen leaves and limbs crunched under my feet. The anxiety in my chest relaxed the moment the dense woods crowded in around me. It felt like being in a fairy realm, free from the cage of my life.

I breathed deeply, taking in earthy scents of soft dirt and flourishing vegetation. Beams of the golden moon sliced through the oaks swaying above me, lighting the worn pathway to Mr. Kingly's grave.

My erratic breathing stuttered, and I wrinkled my nose. The bitter odor of stale water and mud assaulted my senses. Frogs croaked a steady melody of swamp notes, filling the humid air with soothing vibrations. I was almost there.

A black span of water glistened ahead, lining the property's edge. I heaved forward three more steps then released the handles. The wagon slammed into the spongy ground.

I stretched, bowing my back against the strain of my smothering garments. Carting a dead body on a rickety carriage was no small feat, especially when you wore more than twenty pounds of fabric and a corset squeezed your midsection like a vise.

Reaching along my nape, I found the small buttons fastening my dress. I quickly undid the top few and wrangled out of the material until I could slip it over my head. Next, I yanked off my hoops, dropping them on my pile of clothing. My corset came after, then I shimmied stockings off.

A sudden breeze rustled the branches above, and my sweat-soaked skin prickled. I raised my face to the sky, reveling in the wind ruffling through my thin, white shift.

Something splashed the water. I jerked my head to the right where two reflective eyes bobbed to the surface, weighing my threat on its territory. The alligator swam downstream, languid and unbothered by my presence.

It was unfortunate Mr. Kingly would be meat for the monsters of my swamp, but nature was a vicious cycle, wasn't it?

Balling the sheet securely in both fists, I tugged his corpse off the wagon. He thudded to the ground in a heavy heap of lifeless flesh and bones. I swallowed back the nausea working its way from my stomach and paced a slow circle at his feet, gathering what I could of my spine.

I clutched the sheet around his legs and lunged backward, dragging him toward the water. My toes sunk into the wet earth, making sucking sounds every time I took a dreadful step.

Grunting, I leaned back, hefting Mr. Kingly's hundred and eighty pounds into the stream. Water swirled in around him. Another grunt and lunge. His body lightened and I loosened my grasp on the cloth. I pulled again, this time merely guiding him with my fingers. The water welcomed him to her bosom like a delicate feather. The fabric puffed up around him, filling with fluid.

I let go and poked him gently. Mr. Kingly floated away, drifting on a current in the center of the stream.

A second alligator skittered into the water from the opposite embankment. My heart skipped. The silhouette of its large frame snaked out to meet Mr. Kingly, and he plunged below the shimmering surface in the blink of an eye.

Gone was the evidence of my sin, but the waters of the swamp would never be enough to cleanse the iniquities shadowing my soul.

I wrapped my arms around my chest, warding off the chill creeping into my skin. My shift hovered around my knees, wavering in the dark undercurrents lapping at my legs. The rhythmic motion rocking into my thigh comforted me while I surveyed the quiet, glassy swamp. I had to be certain Mr. Kingly would not float topside again.

The sensation of being watched tingled between my shoulder blades. I sunk my teeth into my bottom lip to deter my nerves and slowly turned.

My breath hitched.

A man stood directly behind me, quiet and attentive. The overhang of Spanish moss and branches swayed on the breeze, casting concealing shadows over his face and shoulders.

I narrowed my eyes, straining to see his face, but couldn't define a single feature. Steering my focus downward, I drank in the slick skin of his naked torso. Moonlight gleamed off every hard contour and soft ripple moving in his chest. He drew in rapid breaths and clenched his fists at his side.

"Hello?" I choked out, crossing my hands over my chest to hide my thinly covered body.

How much did he see? Did he witnessed me feeding Mr. Kingly to the alligators?

I lifted my foot from the swampy river bottom and waded forward, hoping the man would step out from the shadows to reveal himself. I hiked up the embankment and paused…waiting…watching.

"Show yourself, sir. It is impolite to watch a lady in her unmentionables and refuse to introduce yourself."

I took another step toward the figure. His chest rose on an expansive breath, then he released a low growl.

Situating my right arm over my breasts, I bent over and bunched the dripping section of my gown in my left hand. I squeezed the water from my hem, feeling his stare track my movements like a wolf would a lamb.

"Sir, I demand you come out and present yourself this instant." I moved one step closer but stopped. The ridges of his body tensed. "This is private property. You should not be here," I scolded.

He spun on his bare feet and sprinted into the forest. The sound of him trampling over dry leaves and twigs soon faded.

I gritted my teeth, yanking my shift up just above my knees, then stomped toward the wagon. I couldn't have kept up with his pace, especially not in drenched clothes.

Curling my fingers around the handles, I hoisted the wagon's weight onto its wheels and swung it in a broad circle to head home.

Chasing after a phantom in the night wouldn't do me one bit of good. It would be a complete waste of time, and hints of gold bleeding into the morning sky indicated I didn't have much of it left. Edison would grow suspicious if I took longer than he thought appropriate for discarding a body. He couldn't know there was an onlooker, or he'd send me to kill everyone within a ten-mile radius.

I scanned the area where the figure stood one last time, biting my lower lip. It was still empty. The tightly raveled knot in my stomach pulled tighter. Surly, they would have stopped me if they saw what I did. Any normal person would have asked, "Hey, you there, what are you dumping in the water?" or even, "What are you doing out here so early in the morning, ma'am?" Of course, normal people wouldn't be lurking in a swamp at five in the morning.

Later in the day, I'd make some pies, carry them to our neighbors, and fish out who my onlooker might have been. For now, I'd have to hope the spy didn't see anything.

A half hour later, I shoved the wagon into an empty spot beside the stables, panting like a dog on a hot day. I gathered my dress and undergarments, fatigue from the day's events settling into my weary bones.

Edison's horses whinnied at me. I held out a hand, skimming over Lightning's nudging snout, then trudged toward the house in the gloomy haze of dawn.

The back door's rusted hinges creaked despite my care opening and closing it. I abandoned my heap of clothing on the floor next to the steps, promising to clean them later. I tip-toed up the rear staircase, and the bleak tension constantly floating through Edison's house knotted the muscles in my neck.

Dragging my shift up, I threaded my arms out and looped it over my head. I wandered through the halls, nude except for the clumps of soil drying between my toes. Edison's bedroom door came into view, and I paused. Stretching my head from left to right, I messaged the tender lump tightening my neck.

I reached for his doorknob but hesitated. Glancing over my shoulder at my own bedroom door, I frowned. Usually, I did whatever it took to avoid spending the night in his bed. Tonight, I couldn't bear to be alone with myself.

I eased into his room and lingered in the doorway, listening for the even breaths proving he was asleep.

He sucked in a puff of air then flopped over on the mattress. A streak of rising sun spilled through Edison's paisley drapes, shining on his closed eyelids.

I tossed my shift on the floor and padded to the wash basin on his drawers. I filled it with water from the ewer then hurriedly cleaned the dirt from my feet. Honestly, I was so tired I could have climbed into bed with clay still lumped between my toes, but I didn't feel like adding to my laundry list.

Strolling to the bed, I released the locks of hair still fixed in the messy bun on top of my head. Soft *plinks* mingled with Edison's snores each time I tossed one of the thin silver hair pins onto his bedside table. I peeled back his covers then slid in beside him and tugged them up under my chin.

He smacked his lips together a few times then rolled toward me. "Everything go as planned?" he whispered sleepily.

Folding my hands over my guilt-curdled stomach, I murmured, "Yes."

A light snore whistled through his nose. He was fast asleep before I even uttered my answer.

I stared at the ceiling, tears streaming down my temples and dampening my hair. The sound of Edison sleeping, comfortable in his peaceful dreams, punched the wedge of resentment deeper into my heart.

Silently, I prayed the night I just ended wasn't the beginning of my ruin.

Silas

I bounded up the stairs and slung the door open, bolting into my house like the porch was on fire. I fell back against the polished oak. The door slammed shut under my weight, and a resounding bang echoed through the quiet foyer. My knees gave out. I slid down in a pitiful mound on the floor.

I should have stayed home. I should have waited until morning to go out. It never does anyone a damn bit of good venturing from their home in the middle of the night.

"Sir, e'rythang okay?"

My somber gaze darted toward the hall next to me.

Hattie, my housemaid, shuffled out, draping a tattered shawl tight around her lofty, slender frame. The soft glow of her lantern flickered across her ebony skin, emphasizing the deep worry creases on her brow.

She pressed her full lips into a concerned frown. Tilting her head to the side, she clutched her shawl close to the base of her neck. "You a'right, Mista Burke?"

I stared up at her, unsure whether I truly was alright or not.

She sat the lantern on the foyer table and squatted by my side. "Lawd, you sweatin' more than I do when I'm out workin' the fields. Whatchu been doin' out there, Mista Burke?" When I didn't answer, she looped her knobby-knuckled fingers around my bicep then gently pulled. "C'mon, sir. I think it's time we get you ta bed."

"I'll be fine, Hattie," I said, patting her hand. Pushing myself up, I smiled weakly. "Don't fret over me. I just went out…for a walk." I peered down at the chunks of earth dried on my feet and ankles. "Why don't you go back to bed. I'll clean the mess I've made here."

"Nonsense, Mista Burke." She rushed to retrieve the lantern from the table then shuffled back to my side. "You go'on get yourself upstairs." Hattie cupped her hand around my shoulder, guiding me to the ornate, marble staircase in the center of the house. "You got meetings in town this afta'noon, papers ta sign, so you can get them crops up and runnin'. I ain't plannin' on being without a job again anytime soon. You just get some rest and let me worry 'bout this mess. I'll have Janette bring you tea in a few hours." She patted my sweaty shoulder, shooing me along.

I obeyed and moved out of her way. Lumbering up the steps, I glanced back at the older lady. I was grateful her family came knocking on my door, looking for work, when they did. They were a loyal bunch and exactly who I needed to help me care for Jenkins' land.

Hattie perched a hand on her hip and sighed at the muddy footprints I'd left on the lush, burgundy entry rug decorating the entrance.

I slugged up the stairs, going through the motions as I'd done a thousand times before. My busy mind jumped from one thought to another while I ambled into my room and leaned against the wall next to my window. Staring out at the last specks of stars fading into the morning, I pondered my reason for returning to Savannah.

Though I felt guilty leaving the mess for Hattie, she was right. I needed to sleep before my meeting with the town's most successful men today. I'd have to convince them my visions for the local businesses were aligned with their's. By the grace of God, I'd managed to claim the trust of Mr. Quinn, or maybe by the grace of his wife and her wandering lust. However, I'd need all five of the partners believing me before I could advance my plans.

Then, there was the new obstacle of Ms. James. Seeing her, standing in the middle of a swamp, I almost forgot my wits. She was so beautiful. She appeared more alive in the dangers of night than when I saw her at Mr. Pike's party.

I was mesmerized by her confidence when she thought she was alone, the strength radiating off her glowing skin. I longed to run my fingers through her rich cinnamon curls, to feel the silky texture of her hair wound around my fist.

And her body…the way her plump breasts peeked through the sheer fabric of her gown like two perfect honeydews made my mouth water. The soft silhouette of her hips, swaying under the water-laden chemise as she moved, seduced me into a comatose fool. Even now, my heart beat faster at the thought of Ms. James, her enchanting form drenched in a sepia moonbeam. I almost swore I detected the dark rose of her nipples and the thatch of cinnamon curls between her thighs.

Edison was not high on my plan's priority, but his association with the partners made him a pawn I'd have to deal with one way or another. Stumbling upon his governess while I surveyed Pike's property certainly changed things, though.

She saw me. She would likely tell him I was there. He'll start to question my intentions and my business, which could ruin everything

I've worked to put in place since I was a child—everything I promised to do since Horace Deveraux left my family with nothing.

I stomped across the room and plopped down onto my bed, flexing my hands into fists of fury. My anger had not waned even a seed's worth in the past thirty-two years.

I blew out a loud breath and licked my dry lips, forcing myself to unwind. Straightening my fingers, I thought once again of the tempting Ms. James...and the body she delivered to the swamp.

Chapter Six

The rooster screamed, jarring me awake.

Edison lay on his side, turned away from me, still sleeping. He'd be up soon. The faint clanking of pots told me Tula was already up, preparing his breakfast.

I eased out of his bed and picked up my soiled under-gown. A damp spot darkened the rose pattern on Edison's rug where my wet shift rested for the past few hours.

I secretly hoped it would leave a pungent odor as a reminder of what he made me do.

Rushing across the hall to my room, I went over the list of tasks for the day. The party attendees left quite a mess, which Tula and I would be responsible for cleaning. We'd have some time without Edison looking over our shoulders while he was in town tending to business this afternoon.

The small reprieves from his watchful, scheming eye were always refreshing.

After washing myself, donning a clean work dress, and fixing my auburn curls back into a tight bun at the nape of my neck, I skipped down the stairs.

Stepping off the bottom step, I halted and smiled, appreciating how diligently Tula worked in the kitchen. She was arranging fresh oranges from our trees out back and eggs from our hens on Edison's plate, precisely the way he liked it. Yes, I'd rather her spit in his food, but that was another matter. Seeing how fast and efficient the girl was at completing chores was satisfying. I taught her everything I knew about keeping a household in good running order, and she learned well.

Someday, she'd make a wonderful wife and mother. I imagined her being hired on under a good family and finding a beau who would make her happy.

Tula picked up an extra orange slice from the counter then popped it into her mouth. Chewing with a pleased expression, she verified everything was just so. Her right hand slipped into her apron pocket, pulling out a small brown bottle with a cork stopper.

My smile faded.

She uncorked the vial, taking a quick sip before she hovered the bottle over Edison's teacup.

"Wait," I barked.

She jerked and shoved the bottle back into her pocket.

I held out my hand. "What is that?"

"Ma'am?" Tula responded. Her green eyes dodged my scornful glare, suddenly too enthralled by Edison's breakfast.

"That in your pocket, girl. What were you going to put in the tea?"

"Nothing, ma'am." She shook her head vehemently.

"I saw you. Don't lie," I grated, thrusting my hand into her apron. Our hands fought in her pocket, grappling over the object. I pried the smooth container from her fingers and plucked it from her pocket.

"No. No," she cried, reaching for the bottle. Her stubborn shoulders deflated. "You'll spill it."

Focusing one eye into the thimble-sized hole, I studied the contents. A brownish liquid swished around the inside.

"Tula," I breathed, worry wrinkles forming on my forehead, "is this…laudanum?"

She nibbled her upper lip. Her head bowed.

The sweet, innocent girl I'd soiled my good name for suddenly broadened her drooping shoulders and blew out a frustrated breath. Her chin lifted high. "You weren't gonna do anything. He got ta be stopped, Ms. James. I cannot just stand by an' watch you kill for such a monster." Tula's chin dropped the slightest measurement, and her hard lips turned down. "They will take you away from me if they ever find out. I don't want ta be without you," she said, her voice quieting on the last realization.

Tears stung my eyes. She was not speaking any truth I hadn't already understood myself. We were the only family each other had.

Heavy boots plodded into the room behind me. I quickly palmed the vial, sealing my thumb over the top, and shoved it into my pocket. Softening my features with the most welcoming smile I could offer, I turned to greet the master of the house. "Morning."

He did not return the smile. He didn't even look in our direction. Sinking into a chair at the servant's table, he grumbled, "Where is my food?" Edison wiped his hand down his face, but it did little to erase the dark circles under his eyes or his grumpy expression.

"Did you not sleep well, sir?" I lilted, pretending to care.

He folded his arms on the table, dropping his head to rest on his forearms. "Is it any of your business, woman? Just get me my damn food. It's bad enough I have a meeting in town, dealing with a bunch of pricks, I don't need your insufferable mouth nagging me in the meantime."

I pursed my lips, staring a hole into the back of his head, wishing I could find the courage to beat him with the cast iron pan sitting on the counter.

"Yes, sir." Rushing to sprinkle salt on his eggs and place a glass of water on the tray, I gave Tula a cautious side glance.

She clamped her lips between her teeth so tightly they were turning white. Her nostrils flared and eyes rounded, darting from my hand with the laudanum in it to Edison's tea.

I cleared my throat, giving her a curt head shake.

From the circle of his arms, Edison asked, "Have you two figured out how you are going to rid this world of Mr. Burke yet?" His tone was calm, as if he was questioning the weather outside today rather than some man's demise.

My heart stopped. A hard pit formed in my throat, trapping a cry of refusal in my chest.

He was serious. He wanted Tula to murder Mr. Burke. He wanted *me* to murder him. This was all so easy to Edison.

He only had to pick the person he wanted gone then threaten Tula and I with pain and loneliness. I'd wilt beneath him like a dying rose, eager to do anything for a ray of sunlight and a sip of water. If it meant living another day in feigned peace and protection from the devils I did not know, I eagerly kill for the devil I knew too intimately.

"Well?" he probed.

I glanced over my shoulder to see his dark, steady gaze eyeing me for submission. His brow hooked upward when I didn't answer.

Without looking away from me, he asked, "Tula, dear, what is your plan?"

Before she could answer, I said, "I'll take care of it. He'll be disposed of tomorrow. I promise."

His lips curled into a devious smile. He knew he'd won with just the mention of her name.

"Good. He can't be allowed to get his foot in the door any farther than he already has. Too many friends inside our business circle will make it more difficult. You have to do it swiftly," he urged, resting his head back down on to his forearms.

I bowed my head, my thoughts swimming in a dizzying array. What was I going to do? I did not want another fallen man on my conscience but letting Tula deal with Edison's new demand was not an option. We could leave him, but he'd find us, and I couldn't take care of Tula on my own with nothing to my name.

Edison pounded the table with his fist. "What in the hell is taking you so long? Is my breakfast ready, or must you go out and gather the eggs still?"

Suddenly, the cool glass tucked in my fingers brought all my thoughts into focus. I uncurled my index finger, considering the dreadful contents. Perhaps, *I* should drink it. Would Edison release Tula then? Could she find another family to work for on her own?

No, he would likely run her into the ground with damning deeds she could never escape.

A light tug pulled on my sleeve.

Through the tears stinging my eyes, I looked at the girl I'd helped raise. Her bottom lip quivered, and her own tears trailed silently down her face. She held out her hand, requesting the vial without words, and nodded encouragingly.

Every worried wrinkle on her forehead, every youthful freckle adorning her damp cheeks, and all the anticipation of freedom behind her emerald eyes begged me to let her finish what she started.

I couldn't have children of my own, but Tula was the closest thing to a daughter I would ever experience. Edison would not tear us apart, little by little, one wicked deed at a time; I forbid it.

Sucking in a trembling breath, I hovered my hand over the cooling cup of tea and tipped the vial on its side.

Half the bottle poured in before Tula wrapped her fingers around mine, tilting it to stop the flow. She wiped the wetness from her jaw and smiled meekly at me.

I stood, stiff as a board, trying to comprehend what I'd just done. Was it enough to kill him? Or would he just sleep for a while?

Tula lifted the tray from the counter and hurried to his side before I could stop her. "Sir, I got some special tea for ya today. It's a bit bitter, but ya hardly notice once I put in the sweet honey from Mrs. Holland's beehives," she said with a tinge of saccharine that made my skin crawl.

Edison's head popped up. He cinched his brows together, studying the murky blush-hued liquid in his cup. "Bitter? What kind of tea is it? Why not my usual?" He sniffed it, jerking his head back and sneering. "I want my lemon tea, Tula."

"Sorry, sir. They all out at the market. I had ta hunt this down. They say it's from a new farmer here in town. Thought ya might like ta be a little adventurous."

I held myself steady, holding onto the edge of the counter with one hand while clutching the half-empty bottle behind my back. Skimming my thumb along the poison-dampened mouth of the vial, I observed Tula's deceit with curiosity.

She fluttered around Edison like this were any other day of hell we endured under this roof. She unfolded his napkin to place it in his lap, buttered his bread, then squeezed the remaining orange half over a short glass, draining it until there was nothing more than the pulpy skin left.

Edison reached for the fresh juice, but Tula patted his hand away. He peered up at her and growled, baring a sliver of white teeth through his scowl. "Don't test my patience, Tula. I'll put your skinny ass right back in that cellar."

She smiled nervously. Her slender finger poked out, nudging the gold-trimmed cup closer to his hand. "Your tea first, sir. Wouldn't want it ta get cold before ya could enjoy it properly."

Edison picked up his piece of bread, pinched off a corner, then shoved it in his mouth. He chewed loudly, eyeing Tula as if her mere existence was offensive. Swallowing hard, he looped his finger inside the cup's handle and lifted it to his mouth.

Funny how, at that moment, my mind homed in on how the pink roses hand painted on the side of the cup was the very hue of Edison's lips. Maybe my brain *was* nearing its breaking point like Tula feared.

My heart jolted to a fast, uneasy pace.

What have we done?

I loved this man once. Did I still love him? No. But he meant something to me in the past, and, perhaps, one day, he would return to the man he was before.

I reached out my hand to stop him. The warning dangled at the tip of my tongue, yet I watched Edison tip his head back and gulp down every last drop of tea in silence.

It was done.

I kept the secret for seconds too long, and now, it was too late.

"There. Are you happy, girl? I drank your awful tea," he spat, hurling the teacup at the wall. It shattered, sprinkling the floor with several milky white shards. He speared a fork into the pile of eggs on his plate and shoveled them into his mouth.

Tula's eyes shot up to me. "Yes, sir. I'm pleased you drank it. I'll remember not ta get it next time if you dislike it so." She scurried around the table, retrieved the broken china pieces from the floor, then returned to my side.

Moments passed while Edison unknowingly devoured his food.

I tracked every move he made and held my breath, waiting.

Chapter Seven

Tula pulled a hot copper pot from the kitchen hearth and carried it quietly through the room. She was careful not to bring attention to herself, lest she interrupt Edison's meal. She poured water into the stone basin at the end of the worktable, glancing over her shoulder to assess Edison's demeanor every so often.

Her leery eyes found mine, and she shrugged, turning one side of her mouth down in a half frown. She continued preparing to wash the dirty dishes and pots, adding soap shavings and cleaning powder to the water.

Edison chewed the last bite of his breakfast, his jaw slowing midway through. The fork fell from his fingers, clattering to the empty plate. His hand slid lazily off the table as if a bundle of bricks pulled it to the floor and he couldn't hold the weight anymore.

My eyes widened. My heart thumped against my ribs. I jerked my head toward Tula. She was frozen, her hands submerged in sudsy wash water. Craning her neck, she watched our house master's senses diminish.

I set the small, deadly bottle down on a cabinet top and raced to Edison. With the same hesitation I would if tugging a cow carcass from one of the swamp gators, I collected his plate and fork. My voice faltered when I asked, "Is there anything else we can get you, Mr. Pike?"

His glazed eyes traced a slow line from my hand up to my face. Edison lolled his head to the side, parting his lips under the heaviness of his lax jaw. His thick, black brows crinkled together, and he stared through me…beyond me.

My eyes stung with the needling of guilty tears working their way to my surface. "Sir?" I whimpered. I changed this man from a strong, dominating being into a bag of mush.

I sniveled a quick breath, strengthening my backbone and forcing the tears away. It wouldn't be long. Edison would be incapacitated soon…to what extent, I wasn't quite sure though.

Did I give him enough to kill him?

Swallowing the lump of remorse in my throat, I moved to take the dishes away.

Edison's hand shot out, clumsily latching onto my forearm. He gave a weak squeeze, which would have bruised me if he had full control of his faculties. "Somethi…," he slurred. His knees eased apart under the table, and his head drooped back. "Something's wrong," he exhaled in a string of garbled words.

His chestnut eyes watered. Heavy eyelids flapped once…twice…then closed.

Finally, Edison relaxed completely against the chair, sagging into oblivion.

I dropped the plate in my hand, letting it smash on the floor. My mouth was cotton dry. Drawing my fingers up to cover my quivering lips, I released a bleat of fear.

What did this mean? Was I free now? Were *we* free? Could we actually leave this God-forsaken house and find our way on our own without him hunting us down?

I spun toward Tula. Her wet hands hung by her side, dripping water onto the hardwoods. She exhaled a deep breath then licked her bottom lip. Her steadfast focus was trained on Edison's motionless face.

My trembling calmed, my shoulders eased down from my neck, and a quiet giggle bubbled up from my chest. I bent forward, bracing myself on my thighs, and laughed. It started slow and unsure but grew to a chest rattling guffaw. Tears spawned from fear moments before were full of delight now.

Tula ticked her head to the right ever so slightly, evaluating my outburst of hysteria. She folded her arms over her stomach, her forehead crinkling in concern. "Ma'am?"

I choked back the last of my chuckles. Gathering a handful of my skirt, I brought the swatch of cotton to the corner of my eye and dabbed the wetness away. "I'm so sorry, Tula." I inhaled a deep breath then sighed. "I...I just couldn't help myself. I'm not sure what came over me. You looked so strange standing there." I lowered my gaze to Edison. "This whole thing is just so...strange." Gulping down the last of my outburst, I collected my composure.

"Is he dead?" The dreadful gravity of the situation crept back into my mood.

Tula stalked to Edison's other side. She paused, scraping her pouty bottom lip between her teeth in contemplation. Her thin fingers reached out, pressing against Edison's neck, searching for a pulse.

She peeked up at me from under long ebony lashes. "What do we do now?"

"Well," my voice cracked, "I suppose we will need to leave. I believe he has some money stowed beneath a loose plank in his room. We could take it and get as far from here as it will carry us. If we stay, his nosey business partners may come to check on him, and we'll only be able to hold them off for so lo—" I broke off mid thought. Pinching the bridge of my nose, I stumbled back until my rear bumped the cabinet behind me. The ground felt as if it were disappearing from under my feet. I sucked in deep, unsatisfying breaths in an effort to keep my wits about me.

"Ms. James? What's the matter?" Tula dashed across the room and fanned me with her hand. "Are you ok? You look as white as an oleander." She yanked a corner of her apron up and blotted the beads of moisture forming on my neck.

"The meeting. If he doesn't attend, they will come calling on him this afternoon."

The girl stepped back, dropping her apron. Her shoulders fell. "We're done for, then?"

I pushed by Tula without answering and lunged for Edison. I thrust my hand into his vest pocket. His skillfully tailored garment ripped. The small square of silk paisley fell away from his breast, and I fumble to catch the thick, silver disk he always carried there.

Edison would be furious when he saw what I'd done to his best vest. I peeked up to see Edison's eyes were still closed. Realizing he may never know about his torn pocket, I grinned and turned toward Tula.

I fingered the small knob at the top of the pocket watch, popping the cover open. Shaking my head, I expelled a breath of relief. "No. We have time."

"No. We don't," Tula said meekly. "He's alive."

The swelling burden I carried through the years as Edison morphed into a monster—the weight which slowly lifted from my shoulders without my awareness over the past two minutes —crashed back down on me.

"You said he was dead."

"No, Ms. James, I asked what we gonna do…if he were dead. I wanted you ta decide how you felt 'bout him bein' gone. If you would be happy or sad over it. You needed to know your true feelin's." She leaned her hip into the cabinet. Staring down at the boot poking out under her dirt-smudged dress, she swiveled her foot back and forth on her toes, grinding an invisible crumb into the floor.

She was right. I assumed it was all over, that Edison was dead. I gobbled up the idea of him being gone and already began making plans in his absence.

I shook my head. "But…I gave him so much."

Her narrow shoulder raised then fell. "I guess it wasn't enough."

My insides cringed at the thought of him living. I crumpled to my knees on the floor, the impact dampened by layers of skirting. Leaning in, I placed my ear against Edison's chest.

Faint, listless heartbeats thumped behind his ribcage, working steadily to maintain his functions.

When I thought he was dead, I almost regretted giving him the concoction, but now, knowing he was alive, I wanted to kill him more than ever.

"I'll give him more." I twisted, looking back at Tula. "Where's the bottle? I'll pour it in his mouth and hold his nose shut. His body will have no choice but to swallow."

She remained silent. Holding her hand up in front of her, she tipped the little brown bottle upside down.

Not one drop spilled.

"It's all gone. Damned thing musta fallen over when ya set it down." Sulking, she thumbed the cork back into the opening and placed the vial back into her apron pocket.

I slapped my hands on the floor in defeat. Puffs of white flour wafted up between my fingers. If he could only see me now. He'd laugh at how desperate I looked, nearly groveling at his feet.

"What are we going to do?" I whispered.

Tula's feet appeared in my peripheral. The young maid, too wise for her years, crouched down beside me and wrapped an arm around my shoulders. She was consoling me when it should be the other way around.

"We could stab him," she offered in quiet resolution.

A sob broke loose from my thick throat. I patted the hand she curled around my shoulder. "No, I couldn't bear to do something so gruesome again. Besides, it will leave too much of a mess. We haven't even cleaned the blood from the cellar yet."

I wanted him gone, but my heart was too fragile to see Edison laying in a pool of his own blood.

"I can get more from Mr. Shen."

I'd heard of the man she spoke of, but never met him. Some of the respectable ladies who mingled with Edison's crowd warned me of Mr. Shen's business. He owned a small house on the outskirts of Savannah where men and women went to smoke their pain away. He enabled their habits of finding a dark bliss in their minds, long after their ailments needing medicinal attention eased.

"Tula, how do you even know about him?"

Her eyes flicked down to a morsel of egg by Edison's foot. Softly, she answered, "My ma. Before she…," her eyes glistened with unshed tears as she thought about her deceased mother. "She spent many days chasing away the pain from the mass on her right breast in his house."

She looked up at the ceiling, blinking away the tears, then continued on a sniffle. "I bartered with Mr. Shen last week when I went for Mr. Edison's suits. Gave him two pounds of our beef fo' that little bit of laudanum. Promised to bring him more after the next butcher. I'm sure he'll give me more if I take him a hog. He was hard up for it on account of a customer killing his only pig. Mr. Shen thought the devil himself possessed the man during one of his smoking sessions."

I stared at Edison's motionless hand hanging limp next to the chair leg. "How long do you think he'll stay like this?"

Tula shrugged, pursing her lips. She studied Edison's softened features, considering my question. "Not sure. I've seen some of Mr. Shen's patrons stay under from dusk to dawn with the right amount of drug. Mr. Pike hasn't drunk laudanum before, so I can't give an accurate guess to what affects it'll have on 'im." Tula picked up one of his fingers, lifting his flaccid limb into the air, then letting it drop again. "Six hours, maybe?"

I nodded, pushing myself up from the dirty floor. "Well, I guess we better get him up the stairs. Hopefully, it will afford us enough time to get more laudanum and take care of his business affairs today."

Holding my hand out to help Tula stand, I settled on my plan to trudge through this horrific ordeal. "Help me get the man to his bed?"

Tula's brows rose to her hairline. "What do you plan to do, Ms. James?"

I waggled my fingers impatiently. She took my hand and rose, brushing patches of white powder clean from her skirt.

I thrust Edison's pocket watch back into his torn pocket, then dug a gold chain holding a small gold token from under his collar. He had the thing specially made last year when he become a partner in Horace Deveraux's clothing company. I unclasped it from his neck then offered it to Tula. "Take this to Mr. Shen. Buy whatever he'll give you for it."

She took the necklace from my fingers and fastened it around her own neck.

I gripped Edison under his arm and pulled. His big body toppled off the chair and slid out of my grasp, landing in a clumsy heap propped against my legs. "Grab his feet, girl," I grunted, straightening him out so I could circle my arms around his torso.

"Ms. James, I'm still not sure how you plan ta fulfill Mr. Pike's business endeavors." She stepped between Edison's long legs and squatted, situating each of his knees along her sides. Looping her hands around his limbs, she gritted her teeth and hoisted his lower half up while I lifted his upper half.

We moved in awkward harmony, lugging him toward the stairs, grunting and panting along the way.

"I will go into town and speak on his behalf. There's no one else who knows his affairs better than me. As much as he would like to deny my intelligence, I learned a lot from him. I watched his every play when dealing with the aristocrats of Savannah. I studied his ploys and understand exactly what he intended to do for the gain of his footing with them. They know who I am in regard to Edison. I'll tell them he's ill and couldn't make it. That he didn't want to inconvenience his peers, so he sent me in his stead."

"But they will stop you at the door. No women are permitted in their meetings," Tula protested, catching Edison's knee from skidding down her hip.

I paused and allowed her to readjust. She was once again right. His band of power-hungry partners never thought much of women intruding in their dealings. They would likely laugh at me, pat me on my rump, and send me on my way.

"Then I will become a man," I huffed.

Chapter Eight

I examined my reflection, noticing every frown line around my lips. I opened my mouth, stretching it into a wide "O" then snapped it shut again. Repeating the gesture several times, I accepted the lines were there to stay and couldn't be eliminated by silly jaw exercises.

Rubbing my fingers along the dark half-moons under my eyes, I blew out an exhausted breath. Merciless signs of my toilsome time with Edison marked most of my features. I pinched a strand of hair resting on my cheek and slid my hand down to the end. Even strings of lightening hair contrasted with my reddish-brown locks, diligently dating me older than my thirty-two years.

The soft slope of my nose and supple arch of my cheekbones had hardened under the southern sun and Edison's constant callousness. Time after time, I'd worn a stern expression to guard my true feelings from him. Perhaps, doing so whittled down my delicate beauty.

I was not a young lady anymore. My better years fluttered away like the dying petals of a Tea Rose. I still detected some of the charm men looked for in a woman, but I would likely be left behind for fresher bodies when gentlemen went seeking a bride.

My eyes trailed down my tall, thick frame. I was a few inches higher than the usual lady's stature. Lengthening my posture and expanding my shoulders, I scrutinized the width of my body. I was a bit broader too.

I could do this. With the right disguise, I could make Edison's business acquaintances believe me to be a man.

Tula came into my room, pinning the end of her black crown braid into place with one hand while carrying a bundle of clothing in her other.

"I wrangled his shoes and shirt off, ma'am. He looks like he's sleeping. No one should be the wiser if they come to call on 'im." She walked to my bed and laid the pile of folded clothes, leather boots, and a brown derby hat at the foot. Her hand lingered on the plain-looking fabrics for a moment. "I ran to Mr. Murray's home and asked Jacob, his farmhand, to borrow his best suit. He's a runt of a man. I thought ya might be similar in size. These are his church clothes, so he'll need'em back by Saturday." She smoothed a hand down her skirt, making herself presentable for the trip into town.

Watching her through my long mirror, I nodded. "Good. Will you…" my words trailed off. I turned, holding out a long, sheer band I cut from one of my old chemises.

She stepped forward, offering a smile that didn't reach her emerald eyes. "Of course, ma'am."

I unfastened the hooks of my corset, letting it drop to the floor. My petticoats and hoops fell next. Tula helped lift my chemise over my head, adding it to the other layers of silk, lace, and stays scattered at our feet. I stood in the center of the room, with all my feminine curves bare, wondering if this was the last time I would feel like a proper woman.

Facing the mirror to take one last glance at myself, I said, "Okay, girl, bind me up." I raised my arms, allowing Tula room to circle around me freely.

She tucked one end between my breasts. I held it there until she could wrap the band around my torso in the first tight loop. Pacing a slow circle around me, she pulled taut on the binding and continued flattening my bosom beneath the strip until she met the other end. "What should I fasten it with?" Tula asked, keeping the edge pinned between her thumb and forefinger.

I scanned over my modest pine vanity. Glittering beside my ivory brush and hand mirror, I spotted my golden swallow brooch. Edison gave it to me when we first moved here. "That," I said, pointing to the small bird with ruby eyes. "You can pin it with the swallow." I gripped my fingers around the band, and Tula retrieved the brooch.

She stuck the tip of her tongue out over her top lip and crinkled her brow in concentration as she secured my binding.

I twisted back and forth before the mirror, assuring there were no tell-tale wrinkles in the band and I was sufficiently flattened.

Tula stepped into view, holding men's trousers. "Ready for these?"

I took the gray plaid pants and stuffed one leg in, then the other.

She reached for the shirt, but I shook my head. "Not yet. There's something I have to do first." I grabbed a pair of silver shears resting at the edge of my vanity. "You can go now. I'll take the carriage into town myself and see you later this afternoon," I said, addressing her reflection in the mirror. I slid my fingers down a small section of my sherry-hued hair until it slipped from my grasp at my waist.

Tula's mouth gaped, and she stared at me with big cow eyes. "But, Ms. James. You can't cut your hair," she pleaded. "It's so lovely. We could fix it in a bun. Them men wouldn't even notice, I'm sure of it."

I spun around, bringing my palm up to cup her round cheek. "These are not stupid men, darling. They will notice, if they look hard enough." Smiling, I gently patted her face. "Please, do what I ask. I must do this alone, or I'll cry and become a blubbering mess."

She gathered a clump of my curls in her fist and held it to her nose, sniffing. "I'll miss it," she admitted, nuzzling her cheek against the silky strands.

"As will I." Tugging my hair from her fingers, I draped it over my shoulder then shooed her toward the door. "Go, now. We have to be fast and clever."

"This afternoon," she confirmed, glancing behind her one last time before she left the room.

Meeting my face in the glassy surface, I shoved aside my pride. I inhaled a deep breath to stifle the sobs rolling up my chest and blinked back the tears prickling my eyes.

"It'll grow back," I promised the woman staring back at me.

Then I butted the scissors inches from my scalp and snipped, welcoming the man emerging in the mirror.

Silas

My carriage rocked over broken cobblestones until the path became dirt where the ride evened out at the end of Cannon Street. Guiding my horse onto Mr. Deveraux's land, I surveyed his mill's appearance and employees.

In the center of the plot was a narrow, yet towering building. Four long rows of windows stacked on top of one another, lining both it's long east and west sides. The glass was clouded by thin blankets of white dust, no doubt produced by the steady production inside.

Behind the building, Ogeechee River drove a fifteen-foot water wheel, powering the machines under Mr. Deveraux's care.

"May I take your reins, sir?" A young boy, ten maybe, squinted up at me from my right. He lifted his hand to his forehead, shielding his eyes from the sun. "Sir? Your horse? I can stow him in the carriage house and water him, if you like?"

I nodded. "Yes, thank you."

My stomach churned at the thought of what this boy endured to receive a meager pay to help his family. I wore his shoes once. Many years ago, on this same land, I ran my legs ragged, tending to visitors and their horses for a skimpy return. I went home every night with blisters on my feet, sunburnt skin, and a growling stomach. Only, I was even younger than this boy.

"Your name?" I asked, noting the worn toes of his shoes and the frayed hole over his right knee.

"Ben."

I tossed the boy a silver quarter, and he swiftly shot out his hand to snatch it from the air. "Feed him some oats while you're at it, please."

When he opened his fingers to see how much I tipped him, his face lit up. His eyes gleamed brightly at the coin shining under the mid-day sun. "Yes, sir. Thank you, sir," he blurted. "I'll give him the best oats we have."

I jumped off the side of my carriage and handed the leads to the youngster. Ben barely reached my waist. I chuckled at his eagerness to fulfill his duty as he tugged my snorting beast, twice his height, away. The horse nipped at his hair playfully.

"You think you can handle him okay?" I yelled after him.

He waved. "Don't worry, sir, I have a knack for making friends of them. We'll be just fine." Ben veered into the cooler shadows of the brick carriage house at the border of the property, toting Domino behind him.

I strolled toward the front of the mill, observing the busy workers tending their duties outside. About a dozen large colored men hoisted full baskets of cotton and indigo cakes onto their shoulders then carried them into the mill. They had broad backs and sturdy legs from years of sweating for Mr. Deveraux.

I followed one of the men inside. A chill snaked up my spine. It had been more than two decades since I last stepped foot in this factory, and little had changed.

Specks of fine lint floated through the air like snowflakes. Lines of spinning machines dominated the cotton-dusted floor, stretching from one end of the establishment to the other.

I covered my ears with my hands, trying to dampen the noise. Needles stabbed metal plates and rickety bobbins spun on thin pegs, creating a constant blend of high-pitched whirring and clickety-clacks that echoed through the large open space. It was hard to keep focus on my purpose for being here.

I swiped at my nose, chasing away a sneeze, while watching children operate nearly every aspect of mill.

A knobby-kneed boy pushed a broom under the feet of a delicate girl stepping up to loosen a hung thread on her machine. The Doffer, no older than eight, hurried toward the spinner on the opposite side, exchanging an empty bobbin with a full one. He smiled, tipping the brim of his Derby hat up in my direction as a polite greeting.

A chubby hand clamped over my shoulder and squeezed firmly. "You finally made it, son," the boisterous man yelled in my ear.

My head jerked toward him. Mr. Deveraux grinned, his gaze casting over his child workers with a glint of pride.

I clenched my teeth behind a gracious smile and nodded. "Yes, sir. My internal compass was a bit mischievous this afternoon. Got lost near the Brady's plantation, then I had to contend with a testy horse as well."

He winked. "Well, glad you made it late rather than never. I'm interested in seeing your plans for our partnership. It'll be good to have some fresh blood in the mix. Those old coots get riled up too easily anymore." He bent closer to my ear, his grip on my shoulder steering me forward to match his steps. "Come, son. I want you to meet the rest of our horde. It's too loud in here to discuss business. One of my girls has prepared freshly butchered pork and sweet potatoes for our dinner."

I dipped my head and patted my belly. "Sounds enticing," I shouted as we walked toward the back of the mill.

In my peripheral, a bow-backed woman hunched over a table, bundling spools of thread into a basket. She paused, bracing herself up on a thin arm against the table, and coughed. Though I couldn't hear her, I knew it was a chest-rattling hack caused by endless days of toiling in this place. I recognized her feeble state because I'd watched my mother suffer the same health until her death.

Suddenly, I didn't feel the hunger I had moments before.

Mr. Deveraux thrust open a rear door and held out his hand, inviting me to exit the factory first. I obliged then followed him down a lengthy dirt path toward his home. Lofty live oaks flanked either side of the path, shading us under their outstretched branches.

We passed several one-room shacks, barely standing. Time shifted their warped, sun-bleached planks until the nails were pulling from the corners and the clay crumbled from between the cracks. Rectangular holes were cut into the sides, letting me see the free men who settled on staying under Deveraux's employ were out to work; only a few women fluttered about their chores inside the small homes.

I tipped my hat to an elderly lady stabling herself on a cane outside one of the shacks. Her skin was glossy and purple like a Black Star lily and glistening with sweat in the mid-day heat. She watched Mr. Deveraux and I pass without acknowledgment while beating a dirt-sodden rug with a branch.

"Never mind her. Ruth's too old to work the fields or the mill, but she's served our family for decades, so I graciously allowed her to stay on my grounds. Her son, Abraham, is a loyal workhorse and promised to pull her weight if I kept her. So far, he's fulfilled his promise."

"I see." How kind of him to give the woman a ram-shackled home with a dirt floor and no door to live in.

"Welcome to my abode, Mr. Burke." Mr. Deveraux led me up a steep set of brick stairs and into his lavish home. Fat, sturdy columns bolstered his porch, adding a bold frame for his well-crafted front door. On the inside, he showcased expensive furnishings covered in elegant silks and azure velvets. Shining gold trims decorating his banisters and tables, indicating he was a man who enjoyed showing off his money. He obviously did well for himself.

My eyes roamed over his extravagant possessions, the need for revenge twisting tighter in my gut. "It's quite impressive," I complimented.

"You could have all this too. Just think about the money we can bring in working together. You'll own niceties such as these soon enough, and you won't even have to lift a finger." He chuckled, ushering me through two ornate French doors.

Deveraux's dining room was alive with the chatter discussing who earned a better return last month and which man convinced their vendor to sell at a higher price. The pungent smell of greed and vanity was thick in the air.

The three stately men engaged in business babble, save for one person leaning against the wall at the back of the room—a youthful gentleman, still quite soft in his frame and face. Perhaps, not too far beyond his teenage years. He kept his silence, perching an elbow on Deveraux's enormous fireplace mantle and taking his fill of the free-flowing information bounding through the room.

His eyes flicked up to mine, and he stiffened, his lips pressing tight. I dipped my head, and he responded by touching his forefinger to the brim of his worn hat. A sudden boom of laughter splintered into the din of conversation, distracting his attention elsewhere.

Mr. Deveraux's partners held tight to their chairs but squirmed anytime someone opposed their arguments about how their trade should be handled or who they should buy from next. Thank God for the oval dining table, almost the size of the room, keeping them separated. They were little more than starving hyenas warring over a feast of wavering fortune. Though they were friends, I had a feeling their camaraderie only ran flesh deep.

"Ah, so nice to have you in our presence, Mr. Burke," the haughty Mr. Quinn bellowed over his peers. He waved his hand, calling me to the empty seat next to him. "Join us. I think you'll like what we have to say." He smoothed his palm over his temple, flattening the greased black hairs that refused to lay down.

I offered Mr. Deveraux a curt, appreciative nod then strolled toward Mr. Quinn. He introduced each man by name and industry specialty as I passed behind them.

"That squirrely gent there is Mr. Clemmons," Deveraux said. Clemmons was a small, slender man with puffy red hair deeply parted in the middle. He had beady eyes and a pointed nose just like a squirrel.

"That rascal is Mr. Adams." Deveraux pointed an accusatory finger at the barrel-chested fellow with slicked shoulder-length white hair. He pulled the pipe from his teeth and held it out toward me for a moment, tipping his head. Seconds later, he clamped his molars around the pipe again.

"And you've met our pudgy Mr. Quinn."

Reaching my position next to Quinn, I took off my hat and bent into a shallow bow. "Nice to meet you all." Before sitting, I tilted my head and addressed the gentleman holding the wall up. "And you, sir? I'm not sure I heard your name."

His eyes slid over the men at the table nervously. He pressed himself flatter against the paneled wall.

"He's just here to represent Mr. Pike," Quinn piped up, deeming the shy attendant an unimportant fixture in the background. "Apparently, the dog couldn't make it on account of food poisoning. I hope it wasn't the cheese he served at his party last night. I have a trip to Savannah in the afternoon and can't afford to miss it," he said, rubbing a circle around his bulging belly. "It's probably best Pike didn't make it anyway. He's really becoming quite the nuisance. Always wanting to commandeer the topic of conversation in these meetings. He forgets he's not the only attainable indigo farmer in the area."

Beyond Mr. Quinn's round head, Mr. Pike's attendant rolled his eyes then dropped his gaze to the floor, mumbling under his breath. He clearly had a different opinion about Mr. Pike's status in this group.

There was something about the slight curve of his jaw and the gentle slope of his nose which drew my focus.

He felt…familiar.

Appealing.

Chapter Nine

Nervousness and disgust warred over my insides, battling to see which would make me vomit first. My stomach riled at the acquisitive ideals of these men.

Deveraux's maids catered dinner into the room, strategically arranging each plate at the center of the table. The simple smell of ham and potatoes made me want to gag.

I took a slow, steady turn about the room, trying to keep my nose out of the tendrils of food aroma floating through the air. Dodging Mr. Deveraux's timid servant girls, I spread my attention over the guests like a fisher's net, listening and learning their status in regard to each other, as well as Edison.

It was no wonder he'd become so ruthless when he threw in his lot with such fools. These men were not trustworthy in the least. Their crude responses to one another on topics they didn't agree on revealed how little they cared about their partners' opinions. This was a battleground more than a meeting room, only with sharp, pointed manners which sustained their false air of civility.

"Mr. Burke, what are your thoughts on bringing in more child workers and expanding the factories production?" Mr. Clemmons called out.

The mere sound of his name hitched my breath.

From the beginning of the meeting, I kept my position far from the table, evading any notice from the attendees. Everyone seemed content with my being there as Edison's eyes and ears, nothing more than a sconce on the wall to them. However, when Mr. Burke came through the doors, the backbone I managed to collect weakened. There was something about his presence that chiseled away at the strong-front I worked so hard to uphold.

I stopped my venture around the room and leaned into the molding of a large window dressed in lace and silk draperies. Peering through the sheer curtain, I pretended to watch several of Mr. Deveraux's farmhands struggle to mend the frame on a broken wagon. The warm tingle of someone's gaze roaming over me heated my skin.

I slid my eyes to the left without turning my head noticeably and caught Mr. Burke's gaze anchored to me.

"Mr. Burke?" a hoarse voice prompted behind me.

Crossing my arms high over my bound chest, as a man might do, I eased toward the conversation in time to see Mr. Burke's head whip toward Mr. Clemmons.

"Uh…yes, sir, I believe expansion in the industry is a fine idea. I'm just not sure why we need to bring in more children. There are plenty of able-bodied adults needing jobs."

The red-headed man to Pike's left flicked his wrist in the air. "Pfft. Nonsense. Most adults will not tolerate the conditions of the mill, let alone accept minimal wages. I say we bring in one hundred more lads and lasses and double their expected quota."

Mr. Burke's jaw ticked so slightly I almost missed it. His eyes dropped to the uneaten food on his plate, removing himself from the outpouring of brute opinions from his peers. He looked like he had a rather large mouthful of words he wanted to add but held back with the restraint of a priest.

"Of course, you'll need to notify Mr. Pike of the importance of his attendance during our agreement signing Wednesday morn...uh, what was your name again, chap?" Mr. Clemmons snapped his fingers in my direction, demanding my attention.

I sluggishly turned to face the table, hesitating to answer. I'd succeeded in saying little during my time in the room, so they wouldn't notice the higher pitch of my voice.

"Your name, young man?" Mr. Clemmons urged, aiming his ear at me to hear better.

I gulped. "Henry," I answered in the lowest timber I could force from my throat. None of the men took notice of my boyish sound.

"Ah, yes, Henry. Make sure Edison knows he is required to attend to finalize this deal. If he cannot make it to us, we will arrange to come to him. As much as we loathe the necessity of your employer, we need his rare dye to finish our production plans. Or so Mr. Deveraux says anyways." Mr. Clemmons harrumphed in Mr. Deveraux's general vicinity and rolled his snobbish eyes.

I nodded, avoiding spoken words.

The tall, hefty ringleader with jet-black hair on top and salted curls at his temple strolled along the side of the table opposite me. He slowed behind Mr. Clemmons, clamping his hand around the ginger's shoulder. "Now, now, we all have our part to play in this empire. You won't mind when you see your coffers growing." Mr. Deveraux curled his lips into a smirk, then slid his gaze to me.

I banded my arms tighter around my chest, warding off the chill he sent over my skin.

All the men in here obviously cared little about anything other than feeding their pockets. Yet, something in Mr. Deveraux's blue irises—that dark glint maybe—foretold of his strangely mysterious ways. He had plans nobody in this room was privy to, and they were all for his own good. It made him an unpredictable animal in this game.

"So, Mr. Burke, what do you think? Will you be joining your cotton crops with Mr. Adams's? We could use the extra material." Deveraux prompted after a detailed discussion of the group's strategy to gain more money.

Leaning back in the chair, Mr. Burke clasped his hands in his lap. His fingers blanched. "Yes, sir, I believe I will."

"Glad to hear it, son." Deveraux clapped his hands happily and gave Mr. Burke a wide smile. "Then, we will see you Wednesday as well."

Mr. Burke dipped his chin in confirmation. He shot out of his chair, placed his top hat on his head, then paused. "Gentlemen, please excuse me. I have other business to attend if the meeting is adjourned."

Mr. Quinn swiveled his head, granting him the reprieve he asked for. The others barely left their banter about the agreement particulars long enough to notice he was out of his seat.

Mr. Burke touched a finger to his hat brim and bid his goodbye to Mr. Deveraux. He raced past me, our eyes locking for the briefest moment, then he was gone. The lack of his presence in the room left me feeling alone, despite the rumble of buffoons lingering about.

After learning who was in charge of what part of the business, I could see the fortune these men could cumulate together. Mr. Adams would help Mr. Burke cultivate his cotton crops. Together, they would supply Mr. Deveraux's mill where his children worked long hours in horrible conditions.

The partners relied on Edison to bring the specially extracted indigo dye. It was unlike any other, and therefore more valuable. His addition would create garments more vibrant and coveted than those bought in the highest fashion markets of England.

Mr. Clemmons owned a company of seamstresses, young desperate women procured from the darkest alleys. He offered them a life of working their fingers to the bone for a copper coin, rather than spending the rest of their days with their skirts hiked up for the next John.

Then, Mr. Quinn would distribute the clothing Mr. Clemmons' ladies produced in only his stores, increasing the rarity and demand.

They would dominate the clothing industry, each taking their portion of an impressive influx of money…if all went as planned.

What they didn't know was Edison currently lay unconscious in his bed and would soon be dead, crumbling their plans to pieces.

"Well, gang, you've taken up my air long enough. Get yourselves home, and I'll see you all tomorrow," Mr. Deveraux announced, opening his French doors.

I studied the mill-owner, trying to figure out his deeper scheme in all this.

He certainly owned more of the workers. He was also the pivot point in the whole ladder. If he wasn't involved, neither side could complete their responsibilities in the money assembly.

There were plenty of cotton farmers if Mr. Adams and Mr. Pike weren't involved. They could find someone other than Edison to fabricate a different dye to use, even though it would take years to perfect. Seamstresses were begging for jobs, so Mr. Clemmons wasn't a true necessity. Mr. Quinn would distribute any goods he could get his hands on.

Mills were harder to find, though, especially with the workhands and capabilities I saw during Mr. Deveraux's tour earlier. He was the most needed person in this bunch.

I trailed Mr. Quinn and Mr. Adams out the door, but a firm hand grasped my upper arm, jerking me to a stop.

Mr. Deveraux quietly watched the men ahead of me cross his foyer and exit his home. His cold eyes fell on me, narrowing to slits. "Tell Edison I expect him to hold true to our deal."

Clearing the lump of fear from my throat, I lowered my tone and replied, "Sir? I'm not sure what you're speaking of. Can you tell me more, so I might be specific for Mr. Pike?"

A light chuckle rumbled past his pronounced Adam's apple. "No need. He'll know exactly what I mean. Tell him, a deal is a deal. She is mine, and I will get her one way or another."

I kept my mouth shut and jerked my arm from his fist.

He adjusted the crooked hat on my head, feigning politeness. "Go along now. He doesn't have much time to get his payment in order."

The bell on Deveraux's grandfather clock struck the hour, it's loud gongs disrupting my silence. It was three. Tula should be back from Mr. Shen's by now, so we could end Edison and leave Savannah in our shadows.

I wrenched my arm from his fingers, keeping my expression unshaken. "Good day, sir."

I set into the stiffest, most shoulder-pronounced, manly walk I could muster, leaving his home without a glance back.

Chapter Ten

My heart raced, thumping in time with my horse's galloping hooves.

"Hyah." I whipped the reins firmly against Hemlock's flank, coaxing him to pull the carriage faster. His onyx and cream-dotted coat glistened with sweat. I knew he was hot and thirsty from driving me so fast, but we were almost home.

He neighed his protest but picked up the pace.

I was torn, thinking about the scene I might walk in on upon returning. Part of me hoped Tula purchased the laudanum and already poisoned Edison while I was gone. Part of me didn't want any of this debauchery sinking its teeth into her innocence. And still, there was a small, feeble piece of me praying I wouldn't go through with killing Edison.

Puffs of dry, red dust drifted up around me as we turned onto the path to our house. The sight of the dingy, whitewashed porch and chipped brick façade made my stomach turn.

The short journey from town to our homestead gave me a reprieve of sorts, a chance to step back from the grave decisions of my life, despite having thought about them the entire way. I was almost able to pretend I wasn't a part of it. Seeing the unkempt plantation home, surrounded by overgrown shrubs and sagging oaks, hurled me back into the reality of things. I was minutes away from having to decide on the fate of another man's life.

Steering Hemlock to the foot of the porch, I jerked on the reins and forced him into a rough stop. He was fussy but abided the sudden bite of his bridle.

I left the reins draped over the front of the carriage and jumped over the side, landing with one knee pounding into the dirt. Gritting back a yelp of pain, I ran up the groaning steps, flung the door open, and rushed inside.

My eyes darting around the silent house for signs of Tula. The fabric binding my breasts seemed to tighten around my chest, squeezing me like a boa constrictor.

"Tula," I called, tearing up the steep staircase leading to the second floor. I slowed when I reached Edison's bedroom door. It was closed when I left, but now it was cracked. I paused, listening for a moment, unable to hear anything over my heavy breaths and the steady beat of blood in my ears.

Panic wrung my throat, matching the tightness banded around my ribs.

What if Tula came home and Edison was awake? What if she estimated the drug's affect wrongly?

I forced myself to swallow, ignoring the sensation of a sand pit sifting into my mouth. I couldn't bear it if Tula was dead.

Curling my fingers around the door's edge, I eased it open enough to see Edison's bed. His body lay motionless under the rumpled blankets. Releasing a breath of relief, I entered the room.

Tula stared out Edison's window, rocking from foot to foot. She wrapped her hands snuggly around her middle.

"I'm home," I said, approaching the bed. My eyes roamed over Edison's slack frame. He looked as though he hadn't moved an inch since I left. "Did you give it to him already?"

She didn't turn to greet me, only continued to sway like a mother rocking a baby. "I been standin' here tryin' to figure out what we gonna do." Her sleek shoulders rose and fell around an exhale of disappointment. "Mista Shen didn't have no more."

I frowned, glancing at Edison. "None at all?"

Tula spun on her boot heel, defeat weighing her youthful features down. She unwrapped a hand from her stomach and held up a tiny sapphire glass vessel, smaller than the bottle she originally purchased. "Had to bribe one of Mista Shen's regulars for this. Luckily, he was half outta his mind and didn't know what I was saying for the most part."

I walked to her, taking the bottle from her fingers. Tipping it back and forth, I watched the spoonful of laudanum roll from the bottom of the container to the chewed-up cork stopping it. "But this is less than before. This won't kill him."

Tula's sullen expression confirmed my conclusion.

"When will he have more?"

She muttered, "At least a day or two."

Gripping the bottle in my fist, I slid Jacob's old hat off my head and plopped down on Edison's bed.

"What are we gonna do, Ms. James?" Tula peered down at me, and a tear slipped from her eye. She yearned for direction, a promise of freedom and security I wasn't sure I could give her.

"We can't wait another day. They want him to sign documents tomorrow." I stared down at the blue vial cradled in my palm. "That Mr. Deveraux...he wants something from Edison. He mentioned something about Edison making a deal, and it seems he owes Mr. Deveraux a woman." My brows cinched together in thought.

"Deveraux?" Tula squeaked, stepping back.

I glanced up, nodding. "Yes. Have you heard of him? He's quite a devilish man if I've judged him correctly."

"Mista Horace Deveraux?" Her bottom lip quivered on the last syllable.

"Yes." I narrowed my eyes. "I believe that is what some of his partners called him. How did you know?"

The peach glow in her skin drained, leaving her a shade paler than normal. She stared down at her dusty boots.

"Tula, what are you not telling me?"

She wiped her palm across her cheek, catching an escaping tear. "I don't wanna talk about it."

"If you can tell me something about the man, I need you to spill it, Tula. He has bad intentions. Not knowing what they are could make him even more dangerous to us."

Her watery eyes drifted up to me. She hesitated on a thought, her mouth slanting. "She screamed for help, but no one came. They just kept takin' her. And beatin' her until she didn't fight them no more." Her nostrils flared on a shaky inhale. "I can still smell the cigars clingin' to their clothes. All these years later.

"I huddled in the corner of our shack, pressing my back into the wooden slats so hard, splinters pricked my spine. She told me to hide, to be quiet, no matter what they done. I was quiet, Ms. James. My mama was quiet too. I think they wanted her to scream and fight. Even when she was torn and bruised, she didn't make a peep. He didn't like it when she didn't do what he told her. His friends didn't like it neither. Masta Deveraux took out his pistol and buried a bullet in her head. They left out the shack, one by one, turnin' their backs on a dead black woman who meant less to them than a bag of grain.

"Masta Deveraux heard me at the end, though. I couldn't help it. I'd held in my sob, strangling myself with it, to the point I might pass out from fear and sadness. I took one shallow breath just when he stepped up to the door, and his ears perked in my direction. He saw me in the shadows and smiled, then followed his friends out."

Deveraux's words made sense now. He wanted Tula. She was a witness who got away.

I rose from the bed and gathered Tula in my arms, holding her head against my bosom. "I'm so sorry, darling. I won't let that happen to you." Her body quaked around silent cries.

There was no wonder why she never mentioned this to me before. Slavery was abolished shortly after Edison took Tula in, but there weren't many who trusted a little mulatto girl over a successful white man.

She must've been terrified. This poor child was destined to be tied to murder in one way or another. In one house, she witnessed it and, perhaps, would have succumbed to its brutality. In this house, she was expected to do the deed herself, if not for my interceding.

"I know," she whispered. Tula looked up at me through glassy emerald eyes. "I know you love me like my mama. I know you'll do your best to keep me outta the reach of evil, Ms. James." She snuggled back into my chest, wrapping her arms tighter around my waist.

Suddenly, my shirt pulled taut around my chest, and something yanked me from behind. I flew backward onto the bed, wedging Edison's body under mine. He felt like a log pushing against my spine.

Tula fell on top of me. She lifted her head, confusion wrinkling her forehead. A frightened squeal erupted from her mouth. Her shocked expression grew wild with alarm. She shoved off me, landing on the floor, and crawled backward like a crab.

A strong arm hooked around my neck. I wheezed around strangled cries, protesting the overpowering force pressing down on my throat.

Tula's shrill scream rang in my ears, followed by Edison's gruff voice. "What did you do to me, bitch?" he slurred, drops of his spittle wetting my cheek.

I opened my mouth to respond, but I couldn't speak.

Edison trapped me against his chest. I kicked my legs off the side of the bed, trying to attain enough leverage to break free. Digging my nails into his forearm, I clawed at his iron grip around my neck and writhed atop his body, bowing my back up then slamming it down. Nothing was working. He was latched on too tight.

My vision blackened around the edges. My strength was leaching from my limbs faster and faster each passing second.

He wouldn't let me go this time.

Through slitted eyelids, I caught Tula crawling to Edison's bureau. She flung his top drawer open, shoved her hand inside, and retrieved his revolver. Clambering to her feet, she pulled back the hammer then aimed the gun in Edison's direction.

Edison wrapped his other arm around my chest, yanking me higher onto him. He used me as a shield, all his vital organs protected by my torso.

"Did you think you would get away with this? Did you really think you could ki…," his words trailed off like a drunkard's did when fighting a whisky-haze.

For a moment, his grip loosened, his head lolled away from my ear.

Drawing in a deep breath, I rasped, "Don't, Tula."

"But, Ms. James," she whimpered, "he'll wake up again if we don't do somethin'."

I knew it was true but shooting the man would only cause us more trouble. The evidence left behind would be too hard to escape. I learned that the hard way with Mr. Kingly. Blood still marked the grooves in the basement planks.

Edison rolled beneath me, groaning in a muddled stupor. His arm slid under my chin again, constricting my air.

I planted my heels into the mattress then lifted my head as much as I could in the crook of his clammy elbow. The instant I felt his warm breath on my scalp, I jerked my head backward.

The cracking sound and warm pool of fluid soaking into my hair indicated I'd broken his nose. Edison propelled me aside, cupping his hands over his face, and groaned in pain.

"Get his wrists," I shouted, flipping over to straddle Edison. Snatching the pillow from under his head, I glanced over my shoulder.

Tula was frozen in place. She glowered at Edison, her lips a thin line of determination, her deep green eyes reflecting years of hate. Though her expression showed purpose and strength, the revolver wavered in her trembling hands.

"His wrists," I commanded. "Help me, Tula."

Shifting her focus to me, she lowered the gun. A wave of relief softened her features. She didn't want to shoot him anymore than I wanted her to.

Edison bucked under me, but I squeezed my thighs tighter around his sides. "Get off me," he mumbled through his bloody fingers.

I covered his face with the pillow, mashing down with all my might. Muffled grumbles filtered through the down-stuffed linen. His hands shot out, blindly shoving my chest one second then clenching my arms the next.

Tula rushed to the bedside, hopping onto the mattress beside to Edison's head. She wrenched his hands free of me, then forced them above his head, anchoring each one with her knees.

Tortured gasps sucked loudly beneath the pillow, diminishing with every breath Edison took.

I sank my weight onto his stomach, making it harder for him to take in the air he so willingly deprived me of minutes before.

Scared whimpers broke free of Tula's quivering lips. She shut her eyes and turned her head to the side but kept her grip on Edison's hands.

"It's almost over. It's almost over." My fingers fisted the lace-trimmed edges, refusing to let him loose, though my stomach churned with the bitter remorse.

My attention veered from Edison's shallow breaths to the sound of heavy boots approaching.

Tula's eyes snapped opened, fixing on the presence looming behind me. Her pupils expanded. She inhaled, opening her mouth to warn me.

A deep grunt resonated through the room, and the shadow of an arm raising skimmed along the wall to my right.

Sharp pain bit into the back of my skull, and stars danced across Tula's beautiful face. My thoughts faded to oblivion. I blinked once then succumbed to unconsciousness.

Climbing up the steps to Mr. Pike's residence, I noted the subtle effects of dirt and heat chipping the robin's-egg-blue paint on his two-story house. The toe of my shoe pressed down on a nail working its way out of a loose porch board. I marched forward, and the board creaked sadly under my foot.

From far away, or to a less observant eye, Mr. Pike appeared to have done well for himself. However, I detected his success was less than his partners at the mill, which meant he could be more desperate than them. Perhaps, I would be able to persuade him to help me. Surely, he'd rather help tear the company to pieces and accrue more profits than wallow for scraps from the others.

I raised my fist to knock on his door. A lady's wail echoed through the otherwise silent home, stopping me.

Pictures of what Mr. Pike could be doing to Ms. James ripped through my mind.

Easing the door open, I stepped inside and listened for sounds of a scuffle, another scream. Muted chatter and thuds came from the second floor.

I raced up the staircase but slowed at the top. Taking measured strides, I clung to the wall, fully intending to catch Pike by surprise. I planned to rush in and save Ms. James from his abusive ways, doing whatever was necessary to stop him. Instead, I witnessed his errand boy holding a pillow over his face, and a young mulatto girl pinning the miserable man to the bed. His feet jerked and kicked for freedom with no avail.

The housemaid's eyes were pinched shut, so she didn't notice me entering the room. Henry deepened his seat on Pike's abdomen, gripping his small fists tighter around the pillow until his knuckles disappeared into the wrinkled bedding.

"It's almost over. It's almost over," he murmured.

I picked up a revolver laying on the chest of drawers to my left and moved in behind Henry. I raised the gun above his head then swung down. The wooden stock pounded into the top of his skull, sending a chilling *whump* through the room.

Henry's rigid spine softened. His head rolled to his right shoulder, and he flopped sideways off Pike.

"No!" the mulatto girl shrieked. She slid over Pike's still body, reaching for Henry.

She glared up at me, tears trailing over her freckled face. "You hurt 'er. Why you did that, mista?" She brushed badly barbered hair off Henry's brow. Hooking her thin arm under his neck, the girl lifted his head off the bed and cradled him. She jostled him gently. "Oh, please wake up."

Sluggish movement at the head of the bed commanded my attention. Pike's head rolled from side to side, his eyelids fluttering.

I pressed the revolver to his temple.

Pike's eyes shot open, fixing on me. His lip curled into a sneer. "I knew you were no good," he garbled.

I glanced at the others stretched across his legs. "Seems to me, sir, you are not in a position to cast judgment on strangers. Now, what would make your help turn against you so ardently?"

"He tried to kill her," the girl blurted, rocking Henry's still form.

"The bitch tried to kill me first," Pike rebutted.

"You deserved it, ya selfish bastard."

"Hush," I shouted.

I was missing something in the midst of their drama. They kept referring to "her." I held the revolver's muzzle firm to Pike's temple and planted my other hand on my hip. Shifting my gaze from the servant girl to Edison, I considered Ms. James's absence and the errand boy's involvement with Pike's affairs.

"You will pay for this, Tula. You and Synth—"

"Shut your damn mouth," I demanded, shoving his head with the gun.

Tula snorted, gathering the phlegm she'd produced from weeping deep in her throat, then spat on Pike's chest. She turned her attention back to Henry. Blood smeared onto her arm from Henry's scalp.

I squinted at the unconscious young man slouched against Tula's chest. His delicate features seemed so familiar to me at the meeting because he *was* familiar.

It was apparent now that his brooding expression was relaxed. The fine arch of his brows, the small blemish under his right nostril, and the moderate flare of his bottom lip. They were the traits which accented Ms. James's lovely features at Pike's party, attracting me like a sailor to a siren.

"That's Ms. James," I stated more than asked.

Tula nodded, raking her fingers through Synthia's chopped hair. "She cut it all off. We had to do something to hold the men off until we could flee."

I saw what Ms. James did with the body in the swamp, and I had a notion of what kind of man their employer was. A person under those circumstances typically ran far and fast.

"I can see why you want to leave this house," I sneered at Pike, "but why go through the trouble of cutting her hair and dressing in men's clothing?"

"They drugged me," Pike interjected.

"Only because we didn't have enough to kill you," Tula grated.

Things began to fall into place.

"Why wait until now to kill him?"

Tula's eyes slid to the side, hate shooting at Pike's sweat-dampened face. "We didn't have enough to put the crude beast down in the beginning, and Ms. James didn't think she could bear to end him with a bloody death." Her gaze darted to me. "Please, sir, don't get the wrong idea 'bout Ms. James. She's a kind and lovin' woman. She just made some bad decisions due to her ties with this man. He would've had us kill you were it not for our efforts to put him in his grave."

"Is that so?" I asked Pike calmly though my insides were raging with hate and disgust. How could a man expect a woman to do such things?

Avoiding my stare, he found a tear in his wallpaper and studied it with great interest. His silence was my answer.

"What were your intentions with him today, Tula?"

"She came home after the meeting, ready to give Mr. Pike his final dose of medicine, but I couldn't purchase enough. Then, he woke while we were talkin' an' attacked her."

"Where is the medicine now?" I scanned over the table by Edison's headboard and his chest of drawers.

Tula gently laid Ms. James down at Edison's feet, slipping a pillow under her head. Once she was convinced Ms. James's head was properly supported, she ran her hands over the thick floral blanket rumpled around them. She smoothed out the wrinkled yellow roses on the cover, pushing Edison's limbs out of the way to search beneath his feet and knees.

Ramming her hand under Edison's left hip, she smiled. Tula pulled her hand out, clutching a three-ounce cobalt-blue bottle.

I pinched the mouth of the container, trying to take it from her.

Her smile fell, and she shook her head, holding it tight. Fear flared in her green eyes.

I nodded, offering her a kind smile. "It'll be alright, Tula. Give me the vial."

In a moment of hesitation, she looked down at Ms. James, perhaps contemplating what her governess would have her do. She released the bottle.

I leaned over Edison, staring him in the eyes. "You are going to drink this. I don't want to worry about you hurting these ladies any more than you already have tonight. Tomorrow, when you sober up again, we will go to Mr. Deveraux's and finish the deal. You and I will take our investments and sign the papers, securing our positions in the company. I will go about my business, and Ms. James will take Tula far away from you."

I nudged the bottle toward him.

Sweat beaded on his brow. His gaze dropped to the glass shining inches from his face. "And…if I don't?" he stammered.

I cocked the revolver above his ear. The clack of the hammer preparing to fire ignited a new dread in his eyes. "I think you best consider my offer."

He gnashed his teeth together, growling in defeat. Snatching the bottle from my hand, he plucked the cork out and pressed it to his lips. Edison poured the drug into his mouth but didn't swallow.

"Drink it, dammit," I barked, moving the gun from his temple to his forehead. I covered his lips with my palm and pinched his nose. "Now!"

He thrashed his head back and forth before finally gulping the liquid down.

Chapter Eleven

I woke to wood squeaking on wood in a steady pattern next to my head. My heavy eyes opened.

A figure sat beside me, swaying in a dark corner of the room—a room that wasn't mine or Edison's. Mr. Burke teetered in an old rocking chair, his face turned toward the last rays of dusky orange receding through the sheer curtains to his right.

Strands of his blonde hair glittered gold with streaks of red I didn't notice before. I marveled at how his hair danced like fire in the dark, or maybe it was my blurred vision creating the halo of flames around his handsome face.

"Where are we?" I rasped, blinking my haze away.

The chair stilled, and his head whipped around. "My house."

I bolted upright, regretting the sudden movement when the room took on the motion of a ship, tossing me to and fro across the ocean. Large hands wrapped around my shoulders, coaxing me back down to the bed.

"No need to be in a rush. You need your rest," Mr. Burke urged.

"Did you...," I winced, brushing the sore spot on the back of my head, "did you hit me?"

Silas sucked air through his teeth and leaned back in his chair. "Well, yes, Mr. James, I'm afraid I did." He reached over and flipped a short piece of matted hair off my forehead. "If it weren't for your new look, I might've realized you were a lady a little sooner."

"So, you just go around, hitting people on the head anytime you come into a room?" I scooted myself up against the headboard, slower this time, and focused on his granite eyes until my head quit wavering.

He chuckled, setting into a steady rock once more. "I do when the person in question is suffocating someone else."

I bowed my head, picking at a looped thread in the comforter covering my lap. I didn't know what to say. He caught me in the middle of trying to murder his business partner. A million excuses wouldn't be enough for him to understand my reasoning behind wanting to kill Edison. In his eyes—any man's eyes—I would be a heartless murderer.

"Tula?" I murmured.

"She's getting some things packed," he said, turning his head back to the disappearing day.

My stomach knotted. She would be sent away, if not arrested alongside me.

I turned away, hiding my dewy eyes. There was a small writing desk on the opposite wall of the room with a blackened ink well and a neatly piled stack of papers in the center. A tall five-drawer chest leaned against the wall next to the door, displaying a crowded collection of whittled figurines. The gray, wool blanket draped over the footboard of the bed and the deer-skin rug warming the floor at my bedside made the quarters feel cozy.

Though the room was mostly empty, it felt quaint...lived in. I wondered if this was Mr. Burke's room, if it was his bed I found myself in, and my pulse thumped faster.

I silently cursed the direction my thoughts were heading and searched his room for a clock. The only thing marking time was the fading light.

A twinge of panic tightened around my throat. I was letting my attraction to him cloud the graveness of my situation. What if he had taken Edison's side? What if they were playing some kind of game at my dispense? What if he already called the authorities?

I lifted my chin, donning a mask of strength and stubbornness. "How much time do we have?" I would not let them take me down, playing the feeble, helpless woman they wanted me to be.

Mr. Burke's gaze darted to me, his bold brows pinched in confusion. "Time?"

I harrumphed, throwing my legs over the side of the bed. The invisible ocean outside the room raged again, jumbling my thoughts, pushing and pulling against my equilibrium. I paused, staring at my feet until the imaginary waves subsided. "Don't toy with me, Mr. Burke. How much time do we have before the sheriff arrests me?" With my eyes on my toes, I eased myself upright out of the bed.

Mr. Burke hopped out of his chair, catching me as I teetered forward. He clutched me to his chest. "I think you need to slow your horses a bit. There's no need for you to get yourself upset and land on the floor with a case of the vapors." The sharp corners of his mouth turned up into a grin.

His nearness and playful, easy manner with me made my dizziness fade.

"I imagine it would make it easier for them to get me out the door without a fight, wouldn't you say?"

The faint nutty smell of brandy lingered on his breath, warming my face with rhythmic inhales and exhales.

His demeanor was cool and collected, not a twitch or a tremor in his whole body. He was holding a murderess in his arms, but he seemed to think he controlled all the cards in his hands as well as mine. Honestly, he did currently have complete dominion over my life and the person I loved most. All I could do was wait and submit to the will of yet another man.

"You have me confused with a different kind of man, Ms. James. I have no intention of having you arrested. In fact, I'd like to help you get away." He dipped his head towards mine, his tongue swiping over his bottom lip to wet it. "You see, I know what kind of man Pike is. I recognize the jealousy in his eyes and his need to control you. It darkens his miserable mind every time he looks at you. I've known many men like him." His hand glided up my spine, cradling the back of my head.

Trying to calm the shiver of need rolling through my body, I gnawed on the inside of my cheek.

I was trapped in his arms, captivated by his eyes. There was nowhere I would rather be. He was so convincing. Maybe he wasn't like other men I've met. There wasn't a trace of deceit on his tantalizing mouth, his arrow-straight nose, nor in his deep-set granite irises.

"And I suppose you're not one of those men?" I breathed.

"No, ma'am, I'm not." His lips crashed into mine, stilling the breath from me and any bit of wit I managed to gain seconds before.

With every eager brush of our lips, every exhale of our heated breaths, each curious swipe of our tongues, I fell deeper into submission. My fingers curled around fistfuls of his shirt, pulling at first then pushing into his hard, heaving chest.

I couldn't do this. It was too dangerous...for both of us. Trouble clung to my back like a cloak of eternal night. I didn't want to burden anyone with the consequences lurking in my future.

On the other hand, if he was not the forgiving, kind man he portrayed, I would be in even more peril. My heart couldn't take his trickery. Regardless of how much yearning he sparked in me, I did not want to be the harlot trading one man's bed for another, only to be baited by a false promise of freedom...of love.

I dug my knuckles into his chest, but he did not pull away. I sunk my teeth into his lip.

He hissed and reared back.

Narrowing his eyes, Mr. Burke brought his fingers to his lip. He examined the blood coating the pad of his thumb, shame flickering across his face. Breathless, he said, "I'm sorry. I've been waiting to do that since I met you. I thought maybe you..." He shook his head and peered down at the floor, a flush of red rising in his cheeks. "Never mind, I shouldn't have assumed that of you."

His arms loosened from around me. I hoisted my oversized men's trousers up and folded my arms around my middle, hoping to contain the molten lust boiling in my core. "No, sir, you should not have." I clumsily toppled to the bed, too weak in the knees and lightheaded from the kiss to hold myself upright any longer.

Mr. Burke lowered to the chair, pressing his toes into the hardwoods. He settled into a persistent rock again.

Someone knocked at the door, breaking our uncomfortable silence. I jerked, twisting to see who it was entering behind me. My muscles tensed, and I stiffened my posture, prepared to bolt past any unwelcome intruders. I would be ready to defend myself against whoever came through the door, no matter how awful my efforts might be in the end.

A tiny voice in the back of my head begged me not to trust Silas. It insisted he would turn me in without a second thought. His words, his caring manner, and the sincerity in his eyes convinced me he told the truth, but Edison taught me a man's promises and actions were not always honorable. Based on my history, I was not skilled at deciphering between their truth and lies, so I would keep my suspicions at the forefront.

An older, dark-skinned woman opened the door. She flashed a motherly smile at me, and the tension in my shoulders relaxed. My eyes roamed over her drab, brown work dress and an apron with bits of food splattered on it while she floated into the room, humming a happy tune. She balanced a tray of white China and a silver teapot on one palm like she'd practiced it a thousand times

"Tea," she chimed, placing the tray on the nightstand between Silas and me.

"Thank you, Hattie. As usual, you have perfect timing." Mr. Burke leaned over the arm of his chair and poured tea into two small cups decorated with button-sized daisies. He dropped two lumps of sugar in one of the cups then crooked his brow at me questioningly. "Sugar, Ms. James?"

I nodded, watching the woman rearrange the pile of blankets at the foot of my bed.

"Don't fuss over that, Hattie. I'll make sure the blankets are unrumpled and Ms. James is tucked in tight before I go." One corner of Silas's mouth tilted up the slightest bit.

Hattie clicked her tongue, waving her hand dismissively through the air. "Don't you be givin' this girl any grief, Silas. She already got enough to worry about without the likes of you causin' her more trouble."

This woman spoke freely with Mr. Burke, like they were old friends. Most servants held their tongues to avoid angering their masters, but there was no sense of superiority looming between Hattie and Silas. I wondered how much he told her, how much of my plight she really knew.

Hattie bent over the bed, dragging her wrinkled hand over the blankets one last time before standing upright. She peered down at me. Her white teeth gleamed behind a wide smile that was nearly too big for her face. Perching her hands on her slender hips, she said, "That's right, girl, I know all about your indecent behavior. Miss Tula been tellin' me all about it."

My eyes grew to the size of the saucer under my teacup. How could Tula be so careless?

Hattie winked at me, cupping my cheek with her hand. "Don't worry, Ms. James, your secrets are safe. I know all about livin' under a man's thumb. I've witnessed more evil than you could ever dream up...and them devils got away with it." She gently patted my cheek and nodded. "I 'spect you had your reasons for doing what you did."

The old maid removed her hand from my face and tapped a finger to her ear. "If y'all need anything, just holler; I'll hear ya. Headin' down to the kitchen to get started on those dumplings you asked for, Silas."

Mr. Burke rubbed his palm over his stomach in small circles. "You're so good to me, Hattie."

"Mm hmm," Hattie mused, cutting him a side glance, "and don't you forget it." She left the room, closing the door softly behind her.

Mr. Burke raised his drink to his lips and sipped, his eyes roving over my face. It felt like he was dissecting me, taking apart my mask to discover my weaknesses.

Suddenly feeling fidgety, I peeled a torn cuticle from my nail and tapped my toes against the plush rug beside the bed. I looked at my cooling drink to avoid his intense gaze.

I lifted my tea from the tray and brought it closer to my mouth, pausing to ask, "What kind of man are you, Mr. Burke? I find it hard to believe you're the type to take in criminals and hide them in your home."

I drank the warm ocher liquid, considering a moment too late they might have poisoned me as I had Edison. He could have easily told his kind maid to slip something into my tea before bringing it up.

He scooted to the edge of his seat, angling his body into my space.

I berated myself for wanting to meet him halfway, for wanting to throw aside all my inhibitions and capture him in a kiss so violent we would both be ruined afterwards.

"I'm the kind of man who will watch a woman bathe in the moonlight, during witching hours, dressed in nothing but her chemise. I'm the kind of man who will stand in the shadows, spying, watching that woman feed a body to the alligators." He inched forward, his gaze locked on mine.

His hand slid up my thigh, dragging along the rough cotton of my trousers. I couldn't bring myself to stop him. My hand quivered, sloshing the tea in my cup. I looked away from his penetrating eyes, setting my teacup back on the tray to distract myself.

Mr. Burke hooked his finger under my chin and urged me to stare into his glorious gray eyes. "Ms. James, I'm the type of man who will take a dangerous woman's secrets to my deathbed, hoping one day she would trust me enough to be mine."

My heart skipped a beat. The brick and mortar I so skillfully layered around my heart over the past few years seem to crumble and drift away like ash scattering in the wind. A lump formed in my throat, and I swallowed, stifling the eruption of raw emotion swirling in my chest. Blinking back the dreadful tears blurring my vision, I whispered, "Why?"

He canted his head to the left, his brow furrowing, as if I were foolish to question him.

I press down against his hand still tucked under my chin, guiding it to his own lap. "Why would you say such a thing?" My voice cracked.

Did I really want to know? He had to be insane to yearn for a woman like me. Or maybe he just wanted to hold my iniquities over my head for his own amusement.

Silas slid to his knees at my feet, separating my thighs with his waist so he could wedge himself closer to me. "What did he do to you?" He studied my pensive features with a wonderment I'd never seen.

I bit my tongue, holding onto my confession.

"I see you, Ms. James. I'm looking at you right now, and I see the loving woman you are. There are few who would murder for a child that wasn't their own." Dragging his fingers along my cheek and tangling them in my hair, he urged me to lean down to him. He placed soft kisses along my cheekbone and temple until his lips brushed my earlobe.

"Do you think yourself a monster?" he whispered. "An unlovable woman?" He gently tightened his hold on my cropped locks and forced me to rest my jaw against his stubbled skin.

He was diving too deep, digging too far down. He was unearthing every one of my buried insecurities, no matter how hard I tried to keep them concealed.

I sucked in a ragged breath, afraid that if I spoke, my insides might spill out for him to see. He would be able to peruse my broken heart, my bruised bones, my fractured soul. He'd pick at it like a vulture, tearing me apart bit by damaged bit.

"Ah, my darling," he breathed, "you are a magnificent beast. I'd be honored to chase you through eternity. A siren demanding my devotion, and I have no problem plunging to my death for a moment of your bliss."

A shudder raked up my body. The honesty and pure hunger in his gravelly voice sent a shock of warmth and dire need zapping through my core. He knew what I did to Mr. Kingly, he knew what I intended to do to Edison, and still wanted me. I felt certain he belonged in an asylum for dismissing my deeds so carelessly, but I was too wrapped up in my own senselessness to care.

"You did what you had to in order to save Tula. You have a good heart, Ms. James. You possess a spirit I could love. Now, I want to save you," he breathed.

I turned my head, capturing his sugar-laced lips with mine. I thrust my tongue into his mouth, frantically seeking the reprieve he offered.

Between chafing kisses, I struggled to address the main concern in his plan. "Edison?" Another breath-stealing kiss. "He'll never let me go."

Silas pulled away only enough to answer, the searing heat of his exhales grazing my face. His lust-drunk eyes bore into mine, flickering with absolution. "He has no choice but to let you go. I have him locked in a room and drugged, hopefully, until I need him tomorrow."

I skimmed my hands down his strong forearms and encircled his wrists. Tipping my head down, I broke the visual connection tying us together so I could breathe and think properly. "Edison is very persuasive. He gets what he wants by any means. How are you so certain he will cooperate?"

He ducked down to lasso my attention back to him. "I'm a persuasive man as well, Ms. James. I plan on bringing his business partners to heel. If he is the least bit intelligent, which I believe he is for getting as far as he has, he will do what we agreed and allow you and Tula the freedom you deserve. In return, I'll allow him to live and continue his part as a paid participant in my company…once I achieve ownership of Deveraux's rights."

My eyes narrowed. "That is your objective? To divest Mr. Deveraux of his position?"

He nodded once, his teeth clenching. "I want to divest him of everything he owns." His gaze flicked to my lips in a moment of…angst…anger…insecurity?

"Why dance with that devil?" I asked, suddenly fearing what future Silas might meet if he continued his risky venture.

I'd seen the unyielding front of wickedness in Mr. Deveraux's demeanor at the meeting. There was no doubt in my mind he'd do whatever it took to keep his hand the highest and richest in this town.

"I owe him," Silas bit out. He dropped his hands from my neck and sat back on his feet, staring at a frayed thread on my trouser seam.

There were a thousand bad memories and a lifetime of pain storming behind his eyes. I decided not to pry further. It appeared he had his reasons, and who was I to argue after doing far worse things than disabling a man's empire.

I cleared my throat, attempting to repress feelings of sympathy for Silas. "So, what do you propose Tula and I do? I have nothing…no way to secure shelter and food for more than a few days." Hints of desperation seeped into my hoarse voice. I squared my shoulders, armoring myself with some semblance of strength on the outside to disguise my true vulnerability on the inside.

When his gaze lifted to my hardened expression, the shadows darkening his face dissipated. One side of his mouth pulled into a soft, knowing smile.

I wasn't fooling him. How could he read me so well already?

His calloused hands engulfed my wringing fists, stilling their nervous twitching in my lap. "I have a fair amount put away. It should get you to the Texas coast. You and Tula can take a ship West. Once you find a place to stay, send word to me. By then, I should have everything finished here, and I'll be able to send you more."

"And after that? Will you stay here, sending me money like a mistress you never see?" I shook my head, my stubborn pride warring with my desire to leave this wretched place. "I can't take your money, Mr. Burke. What if your plans don't come to fruition? I'll be miles away with your money, while you are stuck in a hog's mess…or worse, maybe dead. Do you honestly believe Mr. Deveraux will let you live if he finds out you intend on destroying everything he has? It won't be as easy as you make it sound."

"I never claimed it would be easy. You and Tula will have quite a difficult journey, I suspect. But I will do my best to keep you safe. If it means sending you both away for now, then I'll give you the means to survive until I can come to you. Let me worry about my affairs with Deveraux. I've planned this for over a decade. I promise, he'll get what's coming to him. I'll establish myself here, then join you…if you'll have me."

My mouth parted with silent surprise while my mind toyed with the idea of a future with Silas Burke. Would he be a kind lover? A good man to me and Tula? He was already far more generous than any man I'd known, and he barely knew me.

"It doesn't make sense." I exhaled. "You can't know what you are saying, or you wouldn't be committing to such nonsense."

"I'm quite sure I have a good grasp of what I'm committing to. Like Hattie said, you wouldn't have blindly murdered without good reason. I can see past that damned cocoon you've bound yourself in, you are a good woman. I have rather reliable instincts, Ms. James, and they are telling me you are worth the trouble I might get myself into with you."

I tugged my hands against his, feeling the need to evade his comforting touch. He squeezed his fingers tighter around mine, refusing to sever the threads of intimacy, hope, and infatuation rapidly stitching their way around my heart.

"Trust me," he pleaded, peering into my soul.

I wanted to trust him so badly my chest ached. I wanted to believe his promises, in spite of the nagging voice whispering for me to trust no one.

Taking a deep, cautious breath, I nodded.

Chapter Twelve

I squinted into the blinding morning sun, searching for our path ahead.

"It's gettin' hot early this mornin'," Tula griped, swiping her sleeve across her damp forehead.

Our recent nights were cooled by the early autumn chill, but the days were still sweltering, especially when the sun was high.

"Drink some more water." I nudged the wooden canteen hanging around my neck toward her.

"I'm fine right now. We need to save it for when it gets blistering. It'll get there soon enough." She scanned the green pastures spreading on either side of us. Her hand worked feverishly, wafting warm air toward her face with the small ivory and silk fan Hattie gifted to her for our travels. With each flick of her wrist, the yellow irises decorating the silk fibers mocked me. I knew Hattie painted the delicate flowers for Tula as a sign of hope, but the sour knot in my gut made it feel as though they were taunting me, winking at my foolish illusions of discovering happiness.

I watched Tula fan herself for a moment then lowered my gaze to the spreading sweat spot darkening the back of her gray dress. What was I thinking? We'd likely die out here of heat stroke and exhaustion before we found any kind of proper sanctuary.

We loaded Edison's wagon at the break of dawn this morning. Mr. Burke said goodbye to Tula, and she thanked him for allowing us to stay at his house and for giving us the means to leave Georgia. Before climbing onto the wagon, she threw her arms around his waist and hugged him until I thought he might suffocate.

Tula didn't show affection freely, so this reaction from her made my heart swell more. It was obvious she recognized Silas for who he really was, a decent, trustworthy man.

When it came to saying goodbye to me, he brushed his lips across mine sweetly and told me everything would be okay. I believed him this morning. However, this afternoon, soaked in sweat and slowly dehydrating, I felt a pang of regret.

Edison rose from has drugged stupor an hour before we left. He spied on us from the second-story room Silas secured him in, not moving once while we packed for our voyage. Each time I peeked up at the window, goosebumps rippled over my skin. He wore a cold, stony grimace as a testimony, an oath that he'd find me and Tula, one way or another.

I did my best to ignore him and continue gathering our supplies. I couldn't turn back now; the life I tried to lead with Edison would have destroyed me. This new turn might destroy me, as well, but staying with Edison was no longer an option.

Two buzzards cawed high above our wagon, and I glanced up, the memories of my morning dwindling away. They soared in wide circles, waiting for us to die. The ravenous birds felt like another omen.

If our plans fell to pieces, and the right people captured me, I'd be left for dead, my bones picked clean by those persecuting me.

I clicked my tongue, bidding Millie to pick up her pace and prayed I would not become food for the scavengers.

Maybe their meeting would finish without issues this morning. Perhaps Edison would even abide by his reluctant agreement with Silas, but I knew today would not be the last time I saw him.

Surveying the rough map Hattie provided for us, I vowed to keep my guard up and deal with him when the time came. For now, I would take us as far away from Savannah as I could.

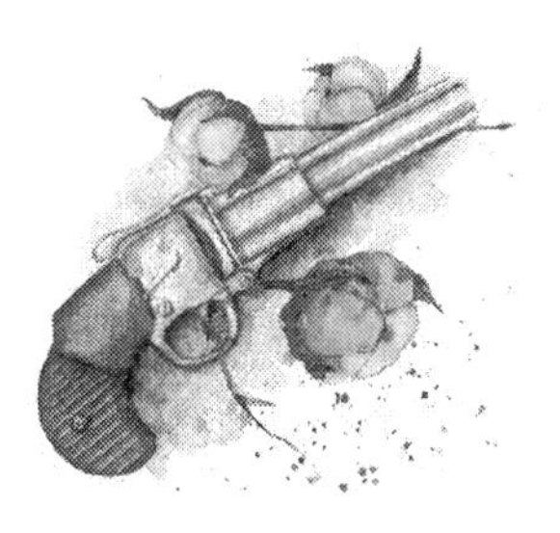

Silas

"Get in the buggy, Edison. If I have to drug you again and carry your pathetic ass into the meeting, I will."

He grinned, shooting arrows at me with his eyes. "I hope you know what you're doing. Once he finds out who you are, he won't take it too lightly."

I rested my tall silk hat on my head, adjusting it so the brim sloped down over my eyes. "They'll be no way he knows. Unless…you plan on telling him?" Waiting for his reply, I took note of his shifting weight from one foot to the other.

He lowered his gaze to the ground, then swiped a finger over the tip of his nose. He was nervous.

"Is there something we need to settle right now, Mr. Pike? Or would you like to keep your stake in the company?"

He glared at me with pure hate. "The first chance I have to take you out of the game, Silas Burke, you better believe I will do it." Smashing his top hat on his head, he climbed up into the carriage and slid over, leaving room for me to occupy the bench next to him.

An hour's ride later, we slowed to a stop in front of Mr. Deveraux's house. His stable boy, Ben, sprinted across the lush grass. He grinned, showing a jaw full of mangled teeth with spaces in between where several of his baby teeth had fallen out. "How are you today Mr. Burke?"

"Fine, fine, Ben. Will you be handling Domino today?"

He stepped back from the carriage's side, allowing me room to climb down. "Yes, sir. May I give him some apples?" He ran his hand over the horse's hind quarters, the flush of excitement reddening his cheeks. Domino leaned his rump into Ben's touch, appreciating the attention.

I pulled a few silver coins from my pocket and held them out for the boy to take. "I believe he'd enjoy that. There's a tip for your extra services. Find my steed some shade," I said, ruffling his dusty, orange hair. "This shouldn't take long."

Ben waited for Edison to clumsily descend from the cab before leading Domino to the carriage house.

I studied Edison, wondering if he'd follow through on his end. "Are you ready?"

He strolled forward, not waiting for me to usher him in. "Let's get this over with," he grumbled over his shoulder. He tucked in the tails of his shirt and straightened his soiled day-jacket best he could.

I trailed the disheveled man up the steps and into the house. The bulk of nearly two decades worth of pain and preparation pressed down on my shoulders. I donned a facade of a proper gentleman's pleasantries and greeted the doorman.

We entered Mr. Deveraux's meeting room. Once again, I was met with the greedy eyes of Deveraux's cohorts.

"Come in, come in," Deveraux welcomed us. He relaxed into a high-back chair at the end of the table, the deep-red velvet trim reminded me of the blood and sweat he'd drawn from his workers through the years. "We were just about to send a search posse after y'all. I think I speak for my partners, as well as myself, when I say we are more than eager to legalize this deal."

The men lining either side of the table nodded their heads, murmuring hums of agreement.

Mr. Deveraux's focus shifted from me to Edison, observing his appearance with a hawk's eye. "How are you feeling, Mr. Pike? You look well enough today."

Edison glanced at me then back to Deveraux. The nape of his short black hair was wet with sweat. He worried his bottom lip between his teeth, contemplating an answer. Massaging the back of his neck with one hand, he said, "Much better today, thank you. Shall we get started?"

Three seats were open at the table, one near Deveraux and two near us, side-by-side. Edison rushed to the empty chair next to Deveraux. He lowered himself in his seat, a glimpse of satisfaction flickering across his snide expression.

I balled my fists at my side, restraining the urge to beat him where he sat, and claimed one of the vacant seats adjacent to Mr. Clemmons.

Deveraux gestured to the man at his right with bug-eyes and a thick, dingy blonde mustache covering his top lip. He sat patiently with a quill and parchment neatly placed in front of him. "This here is Mr. Thrift. He is my personal lawyer and will be conducting this meeting accordingly to make it binding."

Edison shifted in his chair, leaning towards Mr. Deveraux. His gaze darted from me to the lawyer. He rested a shaky hand on the table, polishing nervous circles on the varnish.

Mr. thrift leaned forward, steepling his fingers over the parchment. "Gentlemen, it is my understanding everyone has an investment to make today."

The men groused, digging deep into their pockets.

Mr. Adams pulled out a neat stack of bills tied with a pink ribbon. "This better be as profitable as you say it is, Mr. Deveraux. I've placed a second mortgage on my house to throw in the bucket with you." He eyed his mentor pointedly.

Mr. Clemmons tossed a rolled wad of money onto the table next to Mr. Adams'. "Yes, sir. If Greta knew I sold her family farm to do this, she'd divorce me quicker than a cobra's strike."

The men surrendered their investment, adding to the pile of cash in the center of the table. With each deposit, Mr. Deveraux's eyes burned brighter.

Next to me, Mr. Quinn slapped his bundle of money beside the rest. He pushed back from the table then stood, proceeding to unbutton his trousers and thrust his hand into his pants. He wriggled around, reaching past his potbelly until he found what he was searching for.

The other men gawked at Mr. Quinn wide-eyed and curious, seeming uncomfortable by his undress. Mr. Quinn, oblivious to his partners' judgments, yanked out a velvet bag and dropped it on the table with a heavy plunk. He fastened his buttons again and sat as if everything he'd done was as normal as the sun setting.

His brow quirked up at the other men's surprised stares. "What?" He shrugged a shoulder. "I had a little coin I was hiding from Mrs. Quinn. It is the only way I could get it passed her…that woman has a nose like a hound when it comes to smellin' money," he said, chuckling.

It was down to me and Edison. When Deveraux aimed his attention at Mr. Pike, I stood and reached for the inside pocket of my jacket. "I'll take care of us both." The envelope I filled with mine and Edison's shares slipped from my hand, topping the generous mound of money in the center of the table.

Mr. Deveraux narrowed his eyes at me before turning to Edison. "Why is it you have somebody else handling your business, Mr. Pike? Are you sure you feel up to completing this transaction?"

Mr. Adams piped up. "I'm not sure I trust he has his wits about him, Deveraux." His forehead crinkled. "The man looks pale as a clam. I'd rather he be of sound mind and body when he puts pen to paper."

Edison's glossy gaze swept over me then onto the rest of the investors. He held his shaking hand in the air, dismissing their worried looks. "I'll be fine. The sooner we get this finished, the sooner I can go home and rest. Mr. Burke was just kind enough to help me get here this morning, knowing how ill I've felt."

Deveraux smirked, patting Edison's back. "Alright, gentlemen, let's finalize this contract." He ticked his head at Mr. thrift, encouraging him to take the next step.

The lawyer picked up the parchment and began reading the binding terms of the agreement out loud. Once he finished, he dipped the nib of his pen into an ink well and signed the bottom. "Each of the investors are required to join the agreement and seal it with their signatures." Mr. Thrift slid the paper and pen to Mr. Deveraux, who graciously scrolled his name.

The paper passed around the table, collecting signatures, each partner tying themselves to Mr. Deveraux in hopes of profit.

Mr. Quinn rendered his autograph toward the bottom. He flipped the parchment up between his thumb and forefinger to examine the names. Nodding in approval, he offered the document to me. "Here ya go, son."

I accepted the pen and paper, adding my signature below his. One last signature was needed to make the deal official. Peeking up at Edison from under my brow, my mouth ran dry. An uneasy feeling of betrayal-to-come knotted in my stomach. I swallowed hard, trying to convince myself I didn't see the phantom of a smirk curling his cracked lips.

I rose from my chair and strode toward Edison, contract and pen in my possession. Laying it down in front of him, I rested a hand on his shoulder and squeezed. "Your turn, my friend."

Edison thinned his lips, glowering up at me. Without a word, he picked up the pen, preparing to make his mark. All eyes were on him, eager for the contract to be solidified. He peered down at the document, hesitating, his free fingers drumming against the table.

Mr. thrift cleared his throat. "Is there something not to your liking, Mr. Pike?"

Edison's hand stilled. He lifted his head, pondering the lawyer's question. "I'm not well," he finally confessed under his breath.

Mr. Adams smacked the table, a loud thwack filling the room. "I told you the boy didn't quite look himself. Now what do you propose, Mr. Deveraux? We have all invested. We have all signed. There are shipments coming in and out of port within the next few days. If we don't do this today, we will be losing money."

Deveraux's nostrils flared. The annoyance in his angled brows and pursed lips compelled Mr. Adams to calm himself and sink back into his chair. "How do you mean, Mr. Pike? Do you feel this is just a spell, and we can continue? Or, are you too ill to commit to our endeavor?"

I dug my fingers deeper into Edison's shoulder but kept my silence. I was afraid if I open my mouth, I might expose myself in a fit of rage.

Edison bit back a groan under the pressure of my fingers and shifted away from my grip. "I mean," he growled, "I have been poisoned."

Chapter Thirteen

Silas

"That's one hell of an accusation, Mr. Pike," Deveraux chortled.

Edison risked a peek over his shoulder, attempting to predict my reaction to his statement. "It's true. My governess, Ms. James, and Tula, my housemaid, put something in my tea. They tried to kill me. I'm lucky to be sitting here right now. If it weren't for Mr. Burke, I would likely be dead." Edison bowed his head, playing the part of a poor, pitiful man who was defeated by two women.

He knew I would not confess to taking part in any kind of sedation on their behalf. He understood my stakes in the agreement and how tightly I would hold onto my secret aspirations of undermining Mr. Deveraux.

If I spoke up now, Synthia and Tula wouldn't have a chance. The law would be after them soon, I could tell by the determined look in Mr. Thrift's calculating expression. I needed to warn them before he alerted the authorities.

Mr. Thrift narrowed his eyes at Edison. "You understand the possible consequences of your allegation, don't you, boy?"

Edison nodded quietly, hiding his face in the shadows of shame and weakness. "Sadly, I do, sir."

If the authorities caught Tula and Synthia, they would spend the rest of their days in jail, or worse, they'd be executed instantly.

A fist gripped my heart. It would be hard to live without her, knowing she was somewhere far away—but it would be impossible to live without her, knowing she was dead and I might have been able to save her.

Yes, I had to hold my tongue and let things fall as they may during this meeting. The moment we concluded, I would find her, get her somewhere safe, then come back to take what was owed to me and my family. My attention skimmed over the pile of red and green stamped bills and gleaming coins resting on the cherry wood.

Mr. Deveraux leaned forward, folding his hands together on the table next to my earnings. "What do you suggest we do, Mr. Thrift?"

The lawyer scrubbed a hand over his mouth and meticulously groomed chin hair. "I believe it is safe to go ahead with the contract…if Mr. Edison Pike is willing to sign. Afterward, I will alert the Sheriff. They can question Mr. Pike then take the appropriate steps to arrest Ms. James."

"She's getting away," Edison blurted out, slapping his palms on the armrests of his chair. The muscle in his jaw twitched, betraying the anger he worked so hard at masking behind his helpless façade. He hunched forward, shaking his head. In a cooler tone, he said, "I'll sign the damn contract, but you must hurry. She is already miles away. I want her and that half-breed blacky to pay for what they've done."

Though Mr. Deveraux's features hardened in response to Edison's statement, he quietly slid the pen closer to Edison, permitting him to sign.

Edison quickly scribbled his name and shoved the parchment across the table to Mr. Thrift. "Now, can we get on with finding the murderous bitches?" His play of pity was slipping away fast.

The partners shifted awkwardly in their seats, fiddling with their pipes, readjusting their cravats, and fingering their tamed mustaches. Mr. Adams and Mr. Clemmons murmured quiet judgments to each other, holding their own trial of Ms. James without hearing her account of her actions.

I ground my teeth, gnashing back the fit of anger ripping through my gut. They were all guilty of some degrading unpleasantry. I'd found evidence on each of them for some crude act over the past twenty years. Whether it was rape, embezzlement, or slave-keeping after the abolition, they were all guilty of something. How dare they cast judgement on her? They had no idea what she endured living with this coward.

I didn't really know the details either, but I could sense her constantly shifting between the woman she was and the woman she had to be for Edison. I didn't need an account of all the horrid things that beat her into subservience; it made no difference to me.

I knew from the moment I saw her at Edison's party I could grow to love her more than air. The gleam of mystery in her jade eyes, her quiet confidence, spoke to me. A blossom of infatuation was already full bloom in my heart. If she was the woman of strength, love, and loyalty I detected she was, my heart would beat for her, my lungs would breath for her alone, very soon. She would be my reason for living. I could live a life without obligations of revenge and sorrow haunting me.

Mr. Thrift stacked the signed document atop other papers, no doubt accounting for the investments, allocations of where the money would be spent, and who would control what aspect of running the business. They were all insane if they thought anyone other than Deveraux would hold the reins.

Tapping one end of the bundled papers against the table, Mr. Thrift offered a polite smile to Deveraux. "Looks like everything is in order. I will speak to Sheriff Cunningham regarding Mr. Pike's claims. Don't worry yourself about that affair." He bent over to retrieve a leather bag from the floor. "I gather you will guard the money in your safe as we discussed earlier?" he asked, stowing the contract in his satchel.

Someone coughed on their puff of smoke. The men sat upright in their chairs, drones of surprise and concern fluttering about the room.

"I…uh…," Mr. Quinn stammered, "I was under the impression we were keeping the investments in an account at Savannah Bank and Trust, Horace." His bushy brows pulled up in a worried arc across his wrinkled forehead.

Deveraux pushed up from his chair, loading the money into a large cloth sack. "We will, we will," he appeased, scraping the remaining bills and coins toward him. "I just thought it would be smarter to keep it here for a few days. There's been a slew of robberies lately, ya know. Mr. Grantham nearly has the account set for us all to have access, but until then, it makes more sense to store our fortune somewhere safe…in *my* safe." Deveraux paused, his gaze lifting to study the men surrounding him. "Anybody have any qualms with that?"

Mr. Quinn sank back in his chair. His mustache twitched disapprovingly, but he kept his objection unheard. Mr. Adams and Mr. Clemmons observed each other with leery expressions then gave a single head shake to the man bagging their life's work.

Deveraux turned his attention to me and Edison. Pike nodded, giving him permission to continue.

I flicked my wrist at the sack and tipped my head down, approving his plan. It didn't matter that he would take every cent brought to this table. In fact, he was doing exactly what I wanted. Keeping the money in his home safe would save me the trouble of robbing it from the bank. It would be much easier stealing it from his home…and much more gratifying.

Mr. Thrift rose, retrieving his jacket from the back of his chair. "Mr. Pike, would you like to ride with me to the station? They will want a formal report of your claims."

Edison pushed down on his armrests, grimacing as he lifted himself from the chair. He made quite a show of his feebleness, all to further implicate Ms. James and the damage she'd caused him. "Yes, sir, I believe I will." He shoved the chair backward into my thighs, forcing me to stumble back. "Oh, I'm sorry, Mr. Burke. I'm just so outta sorts, I forgot you were behind me."

I dug my fingers into the leather back of his seat, envisioning wringing his neck. "No need to apologize," I gritted.

He strolled past me, his chin a bit higher, shoulders a little wider, than when we entered Deveraux's.

"I'll stop by later this evening to check on you, Mr. Pike. Wouldn't want you hurting yourself. One might take a trip down the stairs or drown in the tub in your given state."

He turned and glared at me, biting his upper lip to fight the sneer tugging at his mouth. "I appreciate your offer, but I'll be fine. No need to trouble yourself."

I grinned, knowing he'd rather never see my face again. "No trouble at all."

Edison narrowed his eyes then hurried to catch up with Mr. Thrift, who was just crossing the threshold.

He was getting away, but I'd make his life hell soon enough. Right now, I had to find Synthia and warn her.

"If we're done here, gentlemen?" I scanned over the gluttonous men watching the devil bleed them dry.

Mr. Clemmons popped up from his seat. His gaze lingered on the last of his investment as they disappeared into Deveraux's sack "Yes, I believe I'll head home as well. Good day." He tramped out the door, a hushed storm of emotions written on his craggy face.

Mr. Quinn thrust his robust form out of his chair and silently marched from the room.

Mr. Adams gulped down the last finger of amber liquid in his glass then slammed the crystal against the table.

I followed Mr. Adams out, stopping at the door when Mr. Deveraux said, "Nice doing business with you, Mr. Burke." A pleased chuckle burbled from his throat.

He might have gotten what he wanted today, but I would get what *I* wanted before he condemned any more people to the fruitless life my mother lived.

Chapter Fourteen

I scooped up handfuls of creek water and spilled it over our new mare's hind quarters, cooling her off. The remaining traces of red dust ran down Millie's strong legs in thin rivulets. We worked her hard since this morning.

She craned her neck down and lapped up mouthfuls of the crystal-clear fluid like her last drink was days ago. "Good girl," I whispered, patting her muscled rump. She bobbled her head, snorting appreciatively.

I hiked up both sides of my skirt, tucking it under the edge of my corset. A faint breeze drifted under the ruffles of dress, cooling my thighs, and I sighed.

Tula leaned down, splashing water onto her face repeatedly until her skin was clean of the dust kicked up by Millie's hind legs. "Thank God the sun is finally setting. I know I might be destined for hell one of these days, but I like to think I still got some time before that happens. You'd think there was hellfire blazing in the sky as hot as it was today." She plopped down in the dirt, yanking her sleeves above her elbows.

I lowered down beside her, eyeing a copperhead skimming the creek surface several feet away. "We'll need to find some shelter soon. If we stay out in the open like this, we'll have bigger issues than the sun while we sleep."

"Yeah, yeah," Tula griped, laying back on her elbows and closing her eyes, "can't we just stay here for a little bit? We been travelin' all day, and I lost all my urgency to be anywhere but here."

Millie swung her head over, licking Tula's cheek with her dripping wet mouth. Tula fell back, shoving the horses snorting nose away.

I giggled. "I suppose you're not the only one needing a break."

The booming echo of my name being called from some distance fractured my moment of lightheartedness. I jumped to my feet, unpinning my skirt to cover my legs. My name broke across the pasture again, and my heart skipped. "Tula…get the canteen and board the wagon," I ordered, searching the horizon for unwelcome company.

"Synthia, where are you?" A bobbing figure came into view, speeding toward us on a shiny black stallion.

Tula grabbed Millie's reins and quickly climbed into our ride. "Ms. James, we should go," she coaxed, worry apparent in her big eyes.

I gripped the handle on the side of the wagon but hesitated. I squinted, trying to identify the man galloping toward us.

"Ms. James," Tula pleaded, holding a hand out to help me.

I took her hand and hoisted myself onto the seat next to her. The horse back-stepped nervously, thrashing her head against the reins. I peered around the side of the wagon cover, finally able to make out Silas's bright eyes and regal nose.

"Go!" he yelled.

Panic engulfed my chest, squeezing my ribs until I could barely breathe.

Silas flailed his hand in the air, motioning for us to move. Domino sprinted full speed ahead without any sign of slowing.

"Go, Synthia!" he bellowed again.

The rumbling thunder of hooves pounded the ground behind Silas. A red dust cloud floated around three men racing their steeds toward us. They were less than a mile away.

Tula pulled the leather straps, commanding the horse ease away from the creek, but Millie reared up, jolting us backward. She neighed and snorted anxiously.

"Give me the reins, Tula," I said calmly.

She craned her neck around the other side of the wagon cover, realizing why Silas wanted us to move. She gasped, her knuckles whitening around the leather.

"The reins...give me the reins, Tula," I repeated in a more urgent tone, prying them from her iron fists.

I clicked my teeth and snapped the straps against the Millie's flank. She chuffed, but I gained control and steered our rig backward enough to turn around.

Moments later, we were on a steady course south, praying we could outrun the men chasing us. The wheels groaned, and the axels creaked, skipping over every bump and large rock in the road. We held on for dear life, while Millie huffed, sprinting to keep us in the lead.

Soon, Silas caught up to us, riding into view on my side of our wagon. He leaned forward to increase speed, his strong thighs gripping tight around his horse.

"Wh…what are you doing here?" I stammered.

One of our wheels bounced over a hollow in the road, and we lurched to the left. Tula's hand slipped from the edge of the bench and she sloshed to the side. I yelped, grabbing the back of Tula's dress to keep her upright.

"I couldn't leave you out here alone, knowing they'd find you. Pike betrayed you during the meeting." He looked over his shoulder, assessing the waning range between us and the other men. His mouth drew into a tight snarl. "We just need to get you far enough ahead they can't see which direction you go, then we can find somewhere to hole-up for a few days." Silas searched the horizon ahead of us, seeking refuge.

We rode for what felt like hours, but it was probably little more than a half hour. Every few minutes, we managed to gain some space between us and them.

We steered our horses around a tree-lined bend in the road. I twisted to look behind us and puffed out a reassured breath. I couldn't see the posse of men following us through the thick wall of tree trunks anymore. Since I couldn't see them, I prayed they couldn't see us either.

"Over there." Tula pointed to an opening in the woods.

Silas slit his eyes, studying the subtle break in the forest several meters ahead. "It appears to be overgrown, but I think we can get the wagon in there. It might be our only chance to throw them off." He tapped his horse's side with the heel of his boot and clicked his tongue, leading Domino to gallop ahead of us.

Domino whinnied but heeded his master's direction, stomping his hooves to the ground in powerful strides.

Silas slowed in front of the opening, maneuvering his horse in an easy circle. He relaxed into his saddle, hands in his lap, and examined the path. Seconds later, he held up his hand, waving for us to follow, then ducked into the brush.

I tugged on the reins and veered Millie into a slow trot behind Silas. Dead trees leaned against other sturdier trunks, threatening to fall with the slightest shift in wind. Broken branches snapped, crumbling beneath the wagon wheels. Wisps of tall grass and saplings whipped our spokes as we moved like a turtle into the thick foliage.

Silas stopped, allowing us to catch up. "You keep going. I'll be right behind you. Whatever you do, don't stop."

My hand flew out, gripping the side of the wagon. My fingers itched with the instinct to clutch his sleeve and hold him near. "You're not coming with us?" I asked, my voice climbing a pitch higher and doing little to hide my worry.

"I'll be right behind you."

Tula took the reins from me and guided Millie forward through the woods, while I watched Silas retrace the steps we just took.

Once he was close to the main road, he hopped off Domino and bent over, grabbing a large fallen tree. He leaned his strong body back against the weight of the log, dragging it across the path.

I turned away from him, silently hoping he would be quick. The sun was setting. The canopy of leaves blocked out what little light was left of the evening. We pushed forward through the dimming forest, careful to stay where the trees were sparse so we could fit the wagon through.

Acres and acres of woodland shielded us from being found, but I wondered for how long. Even the wind seemed to whisper of my impending fate to be captured, and it was rightfully so. I murdered someone. No matter who was the instigator, or for what reason, I took another's life. I *should* pay. I was no different than any other criminal.

The wagon crawled over a large stone, slamming us down on the ground. Tula squeaked from the impact, bringing my attention back to the reason I disposed of Mr. Kingly in the first place. My daughter, not by blood but by choice. We teetered on the small boulder for a moment as Millie struggled to tug our back wheel over it.

My gaze roamed over Tula's creamy tan skin, wild black hair, and sweet acorn-hued freckles. If I could just get her to safety, I'd have no mind for what happened to me. It would take us twice as long to reach our destination—wherever it was—with two of us in a wagon.

Leaves crunched farther down the trail, cutting into our silence. I laid a hesitant hand on Tula's forearm, warning her to be quiet, and searched the darkening shadows.

My throat thickened, and my heart skipped.

The wet snout of an onyx horse breached the dense mass of pines and snorted. Silas rode Domino into full view, taking our lead.

Tula sighed, blowing a tight curl from her face, and slumped back against the seat. I exhaled and bid my frightened heart to beat at a steady rhythm again.

Silas looked back at us, the heavy sheen of sweat and red flush under his skin indicating how hard he'd worked to block the others from following. "I scouted a ways into the forest. There's a clearing up ahead, and a small hay barn. We should be well-concealed there for the night. I waited where we came in. They continued on the main road, so I think we've lost them."

I mouthed a thank you, yet I couldn't ignore the silent "for now" hanging at the end of his sentence.

Tonight, we would rest in the barn, but tomorrow, I'd turn myself in and trust Silas would get Tula out of danger. Surrendering seemed like the only way to give her enough time to run, to have a chance at a life beyond Savannah…beyond Edison. She could survive with Silas helping her.

Silas ducked under an overlay of leaves, then vanished. Millie towed us through the same brush, delivering us to a pasture of wheat and wildflowers.

We skirted the pasture, cautiously analyzing every sound and movement we noticed until we reached the barn. It was a small building with holes rotted in the wooden roof and dark rain streaks tinting the burgundy sides. Earthy hints of mildew-laden straw and horse hide filled my nostrils, and I sneezed. Tula giggled, but jumped down from the bench without comment.

I threw my leg over the side and paused. Silas's hand clasped around my ankle, grazing the bone just beneath the hem of my skirt. His thumb caressed tiny circles over my stocking. He kept his head down, eyes hidden from me.

I inhaled sharply, my small intake of pleasure-filled breath stealing his attention from my leg. He looked up at me, eyes churning with crazed emotion.

"M…my leg, sir. May I have it back, please?"

A flash of savage desperation and mischief rolled over his noble features. Instead of removing his hand, he whispered, "I'm so thankful I made it to you before them. I…," he glanced down at his wandering thumb, "I'm not sure what I'd do if they hurt you."

I licked my lips, wishing his hand would slide up my calf. "I'm sure you would manage just fine without me, Mr. Burke. You've never really had me anyway. In fact, you'd likely be in a much better position to fulfill your business with Mr. Deveraux if it weren't for me," I said breathily.

He skimmed his palm over the top of my dirty boot and guided it to the step. Holding out his hand, he readied to help me down. "You might be right, Ms. James, but I'm finding you are more important to me than my plans with Deveraux."

Silas lowered me to the grass, fitting his long fingers securely around my cinched waist. He stared into my eyes. "Don't run from me, Ms. James. You can flee Savannah, you can evade the law, but, please...don't run from me."

Tula stepped around the back of the wagon, her fists resting on her hips. "I've taken the food bags and canteens into the barn. It smells a bit foul, but I think it'll do for the evenin'. You comin', Ms. James?"

Silas removed his hands from my waist, and suddenly my skin felt too cold beneath the layers of my coverlets and corset. I cleared the longing from my voice and marched toward Tula, leaving Silas behind. "Yes. We should care for the horses then get some sleep. The earlier we leave, the better."

After an hour or so of feeding the horses and stacking hay bales to clear an area for us to bed down for the night, we all spread our blankets in a row.

Tula tumbled down on hers, yawning. "G'night." She rolled onto her side, facing away from us, and pulled her knees to her chest.

I smiled awkwardly at Silas, butterflies swirling in my stomach.

He lowered himself to his pallet, then peered up at me. His hand lifted, beckoning me to lay beside him. "It's much more comfortable to sleep laying than standing." He grinned.

I rolled my eyes. "Yes, Mr. Burke, I'm well aware." Tugging my riding bodice down, I folded my knees and dropped to the thick pad of straw and wool.

Just before my back flattened against the prickly bedding, Silas scooped his arm under my shoulders.

I jerked my head up, surprised by his gesture.

"I figured my arm would be a better pillow…unless you want to wake up with hay stuck to that pretty face of yours?"

I scowled at him, but he chuckled and waited for me to nestle into his side.

He knew my harshness was an act. He was so confident he understood me, and I hated it. As hard as I fought it, though, there was a thread binding my soul to his. I couldn't ignore it. Our link was almost tangible, growing stronger every minute we were together. It was a shame I'd have to sever it before dawn.

Trapping the inside of my cheek between my teeth and gently biting to hold my peace, I sunk down to the crook of his elbow. I flopped onto my side, facing away from him. There was no need to make him think I submitted easily, so I adjusted his forearm into a position that was more comfortable for me but put a slight strain on his shoulder.

He grunted but didn't protest.

I stared at a sliver of moonlight slashing across Tula's dark ringlets. This was the last night I would spend with her, the last time I'd be within a pebble's throw of the only daughter I had known, and I couldn't even say a proper goodbye.

Squeezing my eyelids shut, I wrangled the rush of emotions begging for release. I traded the bone rattling sobs I wanted to unleash so badly for a single silent tear, breaching the corner of my eye.

As I focused on forcing my insides to heel, Silas's warm hand snaked around my waist. He molded himself to my backside, becoming a shroud of comfort around my cold body.

Warm breaths swept across the back of my neck, sifting through my short curls. I pressed my lips together, blocking the moan rising to my throat. He flattened his hand over my stomach and nudged me closer, eliminating any fraction of space separating us. His heat engulfed me, soothing my ailing heart for the briefest moment.

Caught somewhere between a woman with needs and a rabbit in a cage, I remained still. He didn't say anything, merely held me tight to his chest.

I thought about divulging my life to him in that second of intimacy. I wanted to know him in every way, wanted him to know me. The need to convince him I wasn't the monster I appeared to be gnawed at me. Then I remembered the things he said at his house the night he took us in. It didn't seem to matter whether I gave him my explanations or not. Silas didn't need to be convinced, he seemed to whole-heartedly believe I was a good person.

It was me who needed the convincing. Edison had turned me against myself, made me forget the worthy, desirable woman I used to be. He broke me down and rendered me as the worst kind of thief.

I stole secrets. I stole money. I stole lives.

I stared at Tula's back, bowing around soft snores.

She was my only saving grace. She was my only beacon of light in this miserable life. But my ways were tainting her, regardless if she did the killing or not. She thought it was reasonable to murder Edison when it should have never been a passing thought in her mind.

Unfortunately, I wasn't sure I could be the old Synthia for her again. I wasn't positive I could undo the twisted values I imprinted on her soul already.

She would be better off without me.

Silas's breaths slowed to drowsy, even puffs against the nape of my neck.

I slipped out of his loosened grasp and stood, bidding quiet goodbyes to the young woman I loved and man I was growing to love.

Hoping the two would understand why I left when they woke in the morning, I opened the barn door and stepped into the lonely night.

Chapter Fifteen

I glanced up at the black, velvety sky, wondering if the stars knew my fate. Grabbing the smallest canteen from Millie's satchel, I mentally ran through the items I packed in my bag. The cup-sized canister of water, a meager loaf of bread, and a few pieces of overly dried jerky would be all I needed to get me through my journey back to Savannah. After that, I'd have no use for anything nourishing. I wouldn't last long enough to feel the pain of hunger once the courts were done with me.

Hefting the light bag over my shoulder, I trudged across the open pasture, aiming for the low babble of a nearby creek. Layers of heavy skirting and thigh-high wheat stems made it feel like I was treading water. Pausing in the middle of the field, I hoisted the hem of my dress up my shins and tucked two handfuls of the garment under the edge of my corset. I put one boot in front of the other, testing my new unhindered stride. It was better, but I preferred the comfort of men's trousers.

Mellow wind whistled through the swaying strands of grain. I closed my eyes, blindly walking with the breeze dancing over my face. Soaking up my last hours of freedom, I wished I could sprout wings and magically turn into an owl, flying so high into the sky I could perch on the apricot moon. I promised God I'd spend my afterlife burning in hell for what I'd done, if he draped my skin in feathers. I'd be perfectly content spending the rest of my life, watching over my loved ones with wide, glowing eyes, soaring through the clouds.

God didn't hear my promises, though.

I entered the foreboding forest's undergrowth. Dark, twisted branches drooped low, forcing me to traverse the woods in a zigzag.

I couldn't see any wildlife, but the animals made it apparent they weren't far. Crickets chirped incessantly. Frogs joined the midnight music with deep, throaty groans. Somewhere in the distance, the ominous shaking of a rattler made it feel like the night was snickering at my unease. They reminded me the most dangerous encounters were not always those you saw coming.

Suddenly, my aloneness and the weight of what was to come overwhelmed me. Fear fisted around my throat. I gasped for air, anxiety spreading its prickly tentacles around my chest and squeezing tight.

Tugging at the neckline of my bodice, I broke into a sprint through the woods. The fresh air flooding my lungs had no effect on the panic grinding down on me. I coughed out a wail, then let years of repressed tears poured down my cheeks.

I ran until my thighs burned and my feet hurt. I ran until the creek wound into the woods in front of me, and I couldn't go straight any longer.

Stumbling to my knees, I let my bag slip off my shoulder and plop to the ground. The rumble of rushing water drowned out my cries, washing away the sounds of my pain. I leaned over on all fours, peering into the clear creek water. The reflection of a woman lost to the war of hate, terror, and despair taunted me.

I used to be someone different—a respectable woman with a compassionate heart and kind mind.

Who was this person staring back at me?

A ripple in the creek floated one corner of her mouth up into a wily smirk. I smacked the wavering image of her cheek, dispersing her face into a dozen droplets of splashing water carried away by the current.

Jamming my wet fingers back around the skin-tight, lacy edge of my bodice, I gulped down jagged breaths, and curled into myself.

Rocking back and forth on my knees, I realized steering my fate to Death's doorstep, purposefully, was beyond any reasonable speck of insanity. It was an act deserving of an asylum. I supposed many of my recent acts were though.

Never, in all my years, did I think I would become a murderess. Not once did I think I'd be running for my life, then turning myself in to save another. But this was me now, and I allowed someone to push me down this dark road. I couldn't wholly blame Edison for everything. If I'd just had the strength to tell him no once and for all, Tula and I would be running from just him, instead of the Sheriff too. I hiccupped a cry, the misery in my heart tearing me apart from the inside.

A twig snapped to my right, and my stomach plummeted to my toes.

I jerked upright on my knees, digging my fingers into the ground for purchase. Holding my anguished breaths, I rounded my eyes and focused on the hazy shadows between two trees several feet away.

A tall figure with mussed hair stepped into a beam of moonlight shooting through the leaves. His relieved smile fell into a frown moments after he saw me kneeling on layers of dead leaves in the dewy grass.

"Silas," I exhaled. The intense need to flee relaxed from my muscles. I sniffled, hardening my emotions once again, and hastily dragged a patch of my skirt over my damp cheeks. "What are you doing?"

He moved forward a single step, raking his fingers through his soft gold waves. Turning to look back in the direction he came, he settled his hands on his narrow hips. Confusion crinkled his face.

Silas dropped his gaze, studying the forest floor as if it would magically give him an answer to the question searing his mind. The wheels of uncertainty spun behind his disheartened expression.

He shook his head, his brow creasing in irritation when the answer he found among the dried oak leaves didn't please him. "I should ask you the same thing, Synthia, but I'm afraid I already know the answer."

He slowly started toward me, a flicker of accusation and betrayal glistening in his dark irises. "I thought we had a plan… an agreement. Please, don't tell me you were going to throw yourself at those bloodhounds. You were just taking a midnight stroll about the woods like you did in the swamp, right?"

I sat back on my heels, hanging my head in shame. My fingers tightened around fistfuls of cotton bunched at my knees. "Go back, Silas," I whispered. "Take Tula to a reputable town where she can grow into a civilized old woman with no regrets." I shuttered out a breath of heartache. "Knowing she'll be safe is the only thing giving me strength enough to do this."

He lowered to his knees in my peripheral. I twisted away from him, focusing on a black spider feverishly lacing up a Sphinx moth in the web spanning the fallen branch next to me.

Silas grabbed my shoulders, demanding my attention, and shook me.

I glared at him, angry he followed me, furious he wouldn't leave me be.

His iron hands loosened from my upper arms and slid down to hold my elbows in a more tender attempt to keep me close. "She has no one else, Synthia. I can't be what she needs, and if you're gone, the girl will be alone in this hell of a world. Stay for her." Those observant, steely eyes wandered all over my face, taking in every nervous twitch of my jaw, each doubtful line on my forehead, and the yearning lick of my lips. "Stay for me, dammit."

He jerked me into his chest and crushed my mouth with his. He stole my kisses, one after another, without permission, without care, without apology.

I graciously leaned into him, seeking his consolation like a warm blanket on an icy eve, and opened myself to him. Grasping his shirt, I shoved him backward, his back thudding against the damp earth. He continued his exploration of my mouth—of my soul—while I climbed up his tall frame and threw my leg over his hips.

He tugged down my corset. My breast spilled free, my dusky nipples puckering under the gentle caress of a wayward wind.

I pushed off his heaving chest to sit upright. Peering down at him, I savored every detail of his striking face. The tiny scar slashing through his eyebrow, his squared jaw, the sharp bow of his mouth, it all soaked into my memory like indigo dye bleeding into a fine silk.

Silas's simmering desire skimmed over my surface with the softness of an ostrich feather.

I shivered, my skin welting with gooseflesh. Heat sizzled between my thighs, my body responding to his unabashed hunger.

The similarities of Silas's needy gaze were comparable to a starved man offered his first hot meal in years. His shaking hands, the quick, excited swipe of his tongue along his bottom lip, and his tense muscles reminded me of a panther poising to attack a distracted gazelle.

"I'm not sure what entangles me in your web so tightly, Ms. James, but I'm afraid I'll be caught for life if you allow me to go any further." He reached a tender hand up to my neck and brushed his thumb along my collarbone.

His fingers glided around the curve of my shoulder, making their way back to my décolletage. A mischievous grin played at his mouth. He ventured lower, trapping my right nipple between his thumb and forefinger, then pinched sharply.

Delicious pain zapped through my breast, into my chest, down to my belly, and into the swollen button between my thighs. Slick moisture pooled in my core, soaking into my undergarments like a peach's nectar dripping onto the finest handkerchief.

Throwing my head back, I gasped and closed my eyes. I shut out the glorious starlight to relish the pleasure-pain Silas provoked in my nerve endings.

His low, wicked groan beckoned me from my dreamy haze, and I peeked down through heavy eyelids. The hunger I saw in his expression before was tame compared to the carnal demand crystalizing in his strong features now.

"Then, I suggest you fly away while you still can, Mr. Burke, because I don't plan on stopping you," I whispered.

I dragged the hem of his shirt up his torso, slowly scraping my nails into his flesh. His stomach quivered and flexed under my ministrations.

Silas bit his lower lip and grunted. Traces of a smile let me know he was pleased by the sharp bite of pleasure-pain I returned to him.

Lightening the pressure of my touch, I retraced my path, gliding my hands toward the edge of his trousers. He shuttered. I undid his button, then rose off his waist just enough for him to lift his hips and shimmy his britches down.

He curled up, splaying his hand around my throat, squeezing gently to bring me closer. "Do you feel how much I want you?" he breathed in my ear. He prodded up against my wet folds. "You've haunted me since the first night. All I do is think of you, your she-devil ways, and how I'd like to claim every part of you. Do you know how mad that can turn a man?"

I rocked back and forth in his lap, combing my fingers through the sweat-dampened hair sticking to his neck. "Considering how steadfast you are on having a person like me in your arms, Mr. Burke, I wouldn't dare say you were anything less than a lunatic."

His hand slid from my throat to palm my heavy breast. His other fingers tucked into the back of my corset, anchoring me so tightly to him I'd have to fight to escape.

I didn't want to escape him though. I wanted to be closer. I wanted to crawl inside him, drilling deep to the essence that made him this passionate man, capable of turning a blind eye to my iniquities, and make a home filled with memories of love and devotion beyond anything either of us ever knew.

He devoured my mouth, our tongues twisting and twining with fervid need.

I clawed at my skirt, bunching it up around my waist, then guided him inside me.

As I sunk down on him, Silas's mouth pulled away from me to exhale a faltering breath. His parted lips glistened under the shimmering stars, moistened by traces of our heady kiss.

I held my breath until he was at my end. Pleasure unfurled in me like a blossoming lily stretching its petals beneath a fiery sun. I couldn't expel the air in my lungs or make a sound. I was frozen in passion. A quake of ecstasy undulated up my pelvis, riding through my body like a wave, finally forcing a husky moan from my throat.

Silas's breath quickened. He closed his eyes and fell, slamming his back against the earth. The distress and utter contentment warring in his expression made him look much like a man falling from grace, a man sacrificing his beliefs and livelihood to partake in an instant of glorious debauchery.

In a moment of feeling sorry for myself and needing the comfort of another human, I decided to surrender myself to this man. By the look on his face, though, he surrendered himself to me long before. The unbridled trust he'd bestowed upon me, and willingness to follow me, no matter the consequence, instilled a sense of control and power I'd never had with a man.

My lover's eyes eased open to intoxicated slits, peering up at me adoringly. He kneaded his fingertips into my bare thighs, exploring beneath the piles of wrinkled skirt draping my legs. When his thumbs bumped against my pelvis, he curled his fingers towards my backside, increasing the pressure to better maneuver me. He gripped my hips, urging me into a languid up-and-down motion.

I tossed my head back and vowed to give myself to him. I'd give my whole self, not just for solace, not just for a place to hide during the storm. I'd show him I could be the person he thought I was, the good woman he seemed to find in me. I could be more than the murderess I saw in the mirror, more than the whore who lost her way to please a man.

I could love him.

Silas dug his heels into the ground, rising to meet me on my downstrokes. Liquid heat slickened where we were joined. The all-consuming bliss of release coiled in my belly, climbing to a new height every time he pushed into my depths.

Our pace hastened. Silas's face twisted as if he were chasing something and the elusive object was nearly in his grasp. He was darting toward the same destination I was—Nirvana. Paradise.

My soft moans mingled with his deep, manly groans, echoing into the midnight atmosphere. It was almost as if the lustful noises weren't coming from us but another couple with years of devotion and bedroom familiarity between them. We sounded right together, *felt* right together.

When the smooth, tantalizing friction became too great, my body clenched around Silas, and I stiffened. It took all my energy to continue riding him, milking every last bit of euphoria from our joining I could while the rush of a climax flooded my veins. I cried out to the stars.

My lover throbbed inside me, releasing his own tension with a raspy growl. Trembling beneath me, he jerked out his last few thrusts, filling me with warmth.

I collapsed onto Silas's chest. His heartbeat like a thousand horses galloping against my ear, and I smiled. My own heart felt like it might leap from my chest, but not from exertion. It was the prospect of love which made my heart thump at five-hundred beats per minute.

I did not want to leave this man any more than I wanted to leave Tula.

We lay in silence, our frenzied breaths slowing to match the rhythmic crickets' chirping. He skimmed his fingers in lazy patterns over my spine until I drifted into pleasant unconsciousness.

Chapter Sixteen

An owl screeched above us. My sleepy eyes popped open, squinting at the early morning sky. Sinewy clouds whited out the usual crystalline blue, and a low fog floated over the ground, clinging to the tree roots.

Brushing a crushed leaf from my cheek, I rolled toward the light snoring next to me.

Silas's jaw hung lax, his pink lips fell open around a deep breath, then he swallowed repeatedly as if eating something savory in his dreams.

I smiled, pushing up to my elbow. His palm slid from my shoulder where it was stationed all night, protecting me…or keeping me attached to his side, so he'd know if I tried to run again.

Based on the blot of sun filtering through the glum clouds, it was nearly seven. Tula slept alone in the barn all night. A twinge of guilt poked my gut. If I'd stayed in the barn with them, Silas wouldn't have left her to find me.

Creeping up from the forest floor, I wriggled out of Silas's reach. I slipped off my stockings and laid them across his chest, a sign I didn't leave him to turn myself in. I expected him to bring them back to me. He'd wake soon and hopefully come looking for me at the barn.

I bent down, straightening the bit of his rumpled shirt exposing his lean stomach. He moaned softly, rolling towards me in his sleep. I grinned and scurried back a step. Careful not to make too much noise, I journeyed in the barn's direction.

While I waited for Silas and Tula to wake, I would gather our belongings and prepare the horses. We'd have regular stops to fill the canteens so long as we followed the creek. Another day or two on the road should put us far enough from Savannah's Sheriff to board a room until we figured out exactly where we were going.

Emerging from the trees, I paused, scanning the open field for movement. The eerie night sounds I loved silenced for the day. The tall grass swayed carefree, creating a ripple of gold across the land. Small butterflies flew from one long stem to another, gathering pollen.

I pushed through the lush field and rounded the side of the building. I froze. A tawny horse ate fruit from a pear tree on the other side. Our horses whinnied from inside the barn where we roped them up last night. This was a stranger's ride, saddled with worn leather and well groomed.

Someone shouted inside the barn. It was male…deep and brash in tone. I jerked, my muscles tensing to sprint toward the door, toward Tula. A gun's hammer snicked behind me, and I went rigid. Cold metal pressed into the back of my head.

"Well now, honey, we been waitin' most the night for you. Come on inside an' join us."

The barrel dug into my scalp, forcing me forward. I proceeded the man into the barn, my heart quivering in frantic beats. Flashes of the many ways I might find Tula sifted through my mind.

Did they rape her?

Did they torture her, insisting she tell them information about me?

Would she be dead?

Moving into the barn, I blinked rapidly amid the darkness until the thin slice of light beaming through the loft window helped me see better.

Tula sat on a hay bale in the center of the building, her hands tied behind her back and a filthy, blue rag stuffed in her mouth. One of her eyes was red and swollen. Tears streamed down her dirt-smudged cheeks, and she shivered from the crisp chill of fear.

A tall, wiry man with missing teeth slouched behind her to the right, gnawing a wad of tobacco trapped in his lower lip.

Mr. Deveraux stood an inch from her left elbow, maintaining his presence of aristocratic importance among the three men in the barn.

Tula lifted her gaze. She squealed around the rag in her mouth, realizing I was back. I gave her a weak smile, hoping to relieve some of her panic.

Mr. Deveraux curled his fingers over her shoulder and squeezed sternly, demanding her silence. Tula whimpered her discomfort, wagging his hand off her arm.

Cracking a jubilant smirk, Mr. Deveraux clicked his tongue, never taking his concentration from me. "Would ya look at that, girl. Looks like we found Ms. James without your help after all," he said, teasing Tula. "Or, is it Henry?"

I ignored the guilt jabbing a white-hot poker between my ribs and stepped forward. "Let her go. She had nothing to do with any of this."

"Maybe so, but I can't let her go, ya see. I've been searching for her for a long time. Your dear Mr. Pike found out and was clever enough to strike up a deal with me. Young Tula in return for his partnership." He plucked one of her stray curls, watching the thin strand spring back to her temple. "This girl is mine. I owned her mother, and I own her. Above her mother being my servant and whore, this half-breed is my kin." He sucked his teeth then spit on the ground, shooting Tula a side-glance boiling with disgust. "She is my daughter."

I rushed toward Mr. Deveraux. "She is most certainly not yours to own. She is under my guardianship. Has been for years. And she's more my daughter than she'll ever be yours."

The man with the pistol grabbed a fistful of my hair, yanking me to a stop. He stabbed the gun into my scalp again.

Mr. Deveraux reached inside the lapel of his day jacket and retrieved a folded set of papers. His callus grin deepened. "I kindly thank you for keeping such good care of my Tula, Ms. James, but you will be unable to care for her when you're hanging from the scaffolding in the center of town. Judge Mathis can verify her mother was on my property from 1845, until," he bowed his head, putting on a false frown, "her unfortunate death in 1866."

Tula jutted her chin out. Her brows angled down in pure loathing. She scowled at Mr. Deveraux's contrived attempt to mourn her mother.

"No need fer fermalities, Horace. I 'member Letty's time wit' you clear as crystal," the man behind me said in a mess of words so heavily accented with southern ignorance, one almost couldn't understand him. "She were a sweet treat to behol'." He chuckled. "If I recall correc'ly, 'er bronze skin was smooth like fresh cream."

Mr. Deveraux nodded, staring off at a distant memory. "Yes, Mr. Sibley, she had many fine qualities. Very obedient too. It was a shame she met her end so soon. I quite miss our nightly visits, and none of my other workers could sew a hem like Letty." He shook his head, clearing the recollection from his mind. His oily gaze roamed over Tula's heaving chest. "But, now, I've found my Tula…a little piece of Letty and I bundled up in one very exquisite package."

"I swear to God, if you lay one finger on her…," I spat, trying to yank free from Sibley's clenched fingers. My scalp burned, but I fought anyway.

Sibley hooked his arm around my neck and slammed me into him. In his quick motion to overpower me, he switched his aim from me to Tula. "Keep on fighting, cunt. I'll shoot 'er right here in front of you, then let you hang knowin' she's dead, an' it was all yer fault," he whispered in my ear. "She ain't nothin' but a little negro like 'er whore mama. Wouldn't upset the world one bit to not have her breathin' our air." His elbow tightened around my throat, and I choked. "Jist like you. Ain't no one gonna cry 'cause you gone. One less murderin' bitch in Savannah would do us some good."

I squeezed my eyes shut, gasping for breath, for a way out of this, for a way to free Tula. "Al…right," I croaked.

Sibley loosened his hold. "What's 'at, darlin'? You say somthin'?"

"I'll go," I wheezed. "I won't fight you. Please, don't hurt her."

This was what I planned to do before Silas came to me in the woods—before I gave into weakness and selfishness.

Surrendering to these men wasn't any different than turning myself in like I intended last night. I could try to fight them, but I wasn't sure how much fight I had left. I was weary of running and hoping my sins wouldn't catch up with me…with us. Odds were slim we would escape, anyway. There were three of them, and they were all armed. Tula and I couldn't compete. The risk of them hurting Tula to make me cooperate wasn't worth our minute chance of getting free.

I just prayed Silas would be able to find Tula and figure out a way to stop Mr. Deveraux from harming her.

Mr. Deveraux petted Tula's ebony hair, a toothy grin spreading from ear to ear. "Oh, don't you worry. Tula will be well taken care of in my house."

Sibley wrenched me backward, swinging me around to face the barn door, then shoved me into motion. I lurched forward, glancing over my shoulder at Tula.

The tobacco-chewing cad nabbed her arm and hoisted her off the hay bale. He pushed her in our direction, but she tripped, landing on the straw-covered ground.

Mr. Deveraux lifted his pompous nose, stepping over Tula like she was a log in his path.

His companion pick Tula up by the back of her dress. "You're clumsier than a newly-birthed calf. Watch your feet, youngin'." He spit a string of black tar at her toes.

Tula hopped away, narrowly dodging the spit. A shriek of disgust bleating from her stuffed mouth.

The man laughed then dragged her along. She followed in silence, an expression of defeat hollowing the girlish planes of her face.

Sibley pressed his gangly fingers into my spine. "Move it," he demanded, forcing me into a graceless plod toward Silas's wagon.

I veered right, moving along the bed of our ride. Over the worn trunk of dried food we procured for our journey and the extra blankets we tied in bundles, I searched the far side of the field for any sign of Silas returning.

"Stop right there," Sibley barked.

I halted, obeying his order. I wouldn't dare leave Tula alone with these men if I could help it, so there was no reason for me to run. It would only make things worse.

He snatched my wrists, crossing them at my navel. He unhooked a line of rope from his horse's saddle and bound my hands together. I twisted my wrists, testing how tight they were, but the abrasive threads chafed my skin. Hissing, I wiggled my fingers. Numbness was creeping into my hands already.

I stared across the field, into the ebbing shadows of the forest. Fear compelled me to wish Silas was awake and on his way to save me. Love made me thankful he was asleep on the forest floor, safe in his dreams, where I left him.

I swayed, losing myself to memories of my night with Silas.

Sibley yanked on my ropes. "Keep still," he barked.

I planted my feet firmly to the ground, obeying my captor.

My joining with Silas wasn't perfect—love made on luxurious sheets, spread over hours of ecstasy, backlit by candlelight—but it was what I needed. If I never saw him again, at least I had the memory of how he made me feel and the connection we shared.

The short, precious time we spent wrapped in each other's arms gave me a taste of the love we could have had were I in a different life. It chipped away at the rot Edison spawned in my emotions.

I would hold onto that until my last breath, which I suspected would come soon.

Sibley secured one last loop of rope knotted at my wrists, leaving three feet of the braid dangling at my feet. I grimaced, hissing again from the pinch.

"Awe, I'm sorry, s'at hurt?" he needled, tugging me into his chest. A whiff of stale whiskey wafted from his breath.

My stomach soured. I opened my mouth to dole Sibley an insult, but it stuck in my throat.

Behind Sibley, Mr. Deveraux and the third man hoisted Tula's wriggling body over the other side of the wagon bed. She rolled awkwardly over the trunk and smacked her head against the floorboards, expelling a pained groan.

I moved to help her, but Sibley latched onto my arms, holding me at bay.

"Yer ridin' wit' me. I ain't about ta let you outta my sight. Yer li'l negro will be jist fine where she is. Horace'll take good care of 'er. He'll make sure she has a clean dress fer the week an' all the corn meal she can eat. Hell, he might even let 'er have 'er own pair of shoes, which is more than I think most house girls deserve," he grated in my ear.

Sibley whistled, beckoning his horse to us. The steed trotted in front of me, stopping to wait for his master's next command.

Seizing the back of my bodice with one hand, Sibley bent down behind me and shoved his other hand under my skirts.

I gasped, clinching my inner thighs together. I refused to let this man touch me in such an intimate place.

He rammed his fingers between my knees, ensnaring my leg in a hold that could strangle a snake. His rough fingers dug into my tender skin like gravel, rubbing me raw wherever he touched. My tired muscles quaked from the struggle to stop his advance into my nether regions. I whimpered, sewing my lips together, denying the wail building in my chest.

One of his jagged nails scraped my flesh, causing my resolve to weaken for a single moment. I flinched, and it was all he needed. He hooked his arm around my groin. He lifted me into the air and slung me over the horse's back. I released a defiant yelp.

Sibley ducked beside the horse, reaching for the loose end of my bindings. He looped the long stretch of rope under the horse's belly, tying it in a knot between my ankles.

Fastening my hands to my feet guaranteed I wouldn't slip off the horse and run away, but it was damned uncomfortable for me. Sibley made it clear he didn't care about my comfort, though.

"That should do ya," he said, slapping my rear.

Glowering at a horseshoe imprinted in the dirt, I cursed the wooziness and blood rushing to my head. The horse shifted, and Sibley's scuffed boot pushed through the saddle's stirrup next to my shoulder.

"If I ever get free, you better pray I don't find you," I warned.

Sibley chuckled, leaning forward over my back. "I'll be sure ta hide all my tea, but I don't think you'll be gettin' loose anytime soon, Henry." With that, he gathered his reins, snapping them through the air like a whip.

The leather straps bit into my neck, a painful blow I was sure the ruthless man did on purpose. An acute flourish of heat spread across my bare skin, welting the tender flesh below my cropped hairline. I shrieked, frightening the horse into a speedy gallop.

Sibley steered him toward the main road, laughing, as I jounced awkwardly on the horse's spine.

I turn my head, searching for Tula, my vision bouncing with my body. Mr. Deveraux trailed behind us in Silas's wagon with Tula in tow. The third man rode his own horse while leading the tawny, pear-eating steed.

We were almost out of the meadow when I heard Silas yelling my name. I lifted my head from the horse's round side and scanned the field.

He was halfway to the barn, sprinting through the tall grass. "Synthia," he bellowed again.

The third man twisted in his saddle, aimed a gun at Silas, and fired.

"No!" I squeezed my eyes shut, too afraid to see Silas hurt, and burrowed my face into the horse's flank. Silas wasn't calling me anymore. Echoes of the shot pulsated in my ears, filling his heavy silence.

I whipped my head back toward the area where Silas was running. The silhouette of his body peeked through the swaying grass like he was asleep in the lush meadow. He lay more still than the surface of a frozen lake.

My heart shattered—a fragile, glass organ, splintering into a million tiny pieces in a single fragment of time. My blood ran cold. An anguished scream burbled from my throat, chased by vomit.

A knife was slicing my heart open, filleting it into tiny bits for all my enemies to see.

I hung over the horse, retching on each thrust downward.

I wouldn't see Tula or Silas again.

White-hot pain shot through my thigh like an arrow. I fell to the ground. The piercing ring of gunfire faded, and my ears filled with a rapid w*homp...whomp...whomp* from the blood beating against my eardrums. I rolled onto my side, gritting my teeth together to hold back a groan. I would not give those assholes the satisfaction of knowing they hurt me.

The pounding of horse hooves and a squeaky wagon wheel grew farther away, along with my chance to save Synthia and Tula. I curled up from the cool dirt, wincing from the sharp pain in my leg. Their convoy was out of sight, the only evidence of which direction they headed was dust motes swirling in the air and some low-hanging branches left waving over the path leading to the main road.

Domino darted from inside the barn, trotting to my side. He nudged me with his nose and snorted, encouraging me to find my feet.

"I got it, dammit," I snapped, pushing his wet snout away.

Blood seeped through the singed hole in my pants, creating an expanding, dark blob on the outside of my thigh. I grazed my finger along the second dark blob spreading over the inside of my thigh. Since the shot hit muscle and made it out the other side, I should be okay. Didn't make it smart any less, though.

I unbuckled my belt, yanking the leather strip loose from my britches, and refastened it around my upper leg to stanch the bleeding. Folding my good knee under me, I forced myself to stand. "Son-of-a…" I clenched my jaw, waiting until the stab of pain eased from a mind-splitting fury to a tolerable roar in my muscle.

Hobbling a step toward Domino's side, I grabbed the horn of my saddle.

This was gonna hurt.

Stuffing one boot into the stirrup, I jumped off my stable leg and pulled myself onto my horse without laying too much weight on my injury.

Domino jerked his head, stamping his hind hooves in place while adjusting to my added heft on his back.

I gathered the reins, whipping them gently, and clicked my tongue. Domino dashed forward, already sensing where I wanted to go. He galloped hard, following Millie's trail like a hound dog with a blood scent.

I wasn't sure I could reach Synthia before the bounties handed her over to the Sheriff. I needed to do something to convince the judge to release her, and I didn't have much time to do so.

The courts wouldn't want a lady murderer dangling over their heads, disrupting proper Savannah life; they'd want Synthia punished as quickly as possible. The aristocrats of Georgia would pull their investments in our town faster than the judge could blink, especially if it meant their women might take notice and get the notion to follow Synthia's example.

No, they would not stand for such a spectacle.

Judge Mathis was not one to consider the situation before laying down *his* law either. He'd sooner see her hang than consider her reasons for committing the crime in the first place. They were all more monsters then she could ever be. I saw her kindness the moment I met her jade eyes. I saw past the damnation tormenting her and recognized the strong, loving woman she was. It was buried deep, but it was there.

I would not let her pay for Edison's faults. He was the one who started all this. He would be the one to end it.

Chapter Seventeen

We had traveled all day. The sky opened its gullet around twilight, releasing a steady downpour of rain. A cool layer of water soaked through my dress and corset, making my shift a sopping layer of cloth. My skin wrinkled like a prune from being wet and cold for so long.

I shivered uncontrollably. My teeth chattered until my jaw was too tired to move anymore. Every muscle in my body ached and whined from hours of hanging over the back of a horse. I hadn't taken a proper breath since they slung me atop this beast, and my ribs felt bruised from the constant impact of slamming into its spine every time its hooves met the ground.

To occupy my mind, I counted the rivulets of rain wicking down the short, wet curls stuck to my forehead before they flew away in the wind. Echoes of exhaustion and worry still lingered by the time I tallied droplet six hundred ninety-two, so I gave up.

I squinted at the blur of sodden ground, saving my eyes from the splatters of clay the horse kicked up during our journey back to Savannah.

The reins bit into my back, tightening across my bowed spine. I groaned, grinding my teeth together. The pathway became clearer, the rocks and wagon tracks more distinguishable. Sibley's steed was slowing.

"Whoa," Sibley bellowed.

His horse danced in place, releasing the continuous momentum it bound in its muscles for so long.

The squeak of wooden wheels slowing pierced my ears, and Silas's wagon crept into my limited field of vision.

Everyone was quiet.

Tula was quiet.

Curling off the horse's side, I stretched my neck up, searching frantically for some sign they didn't abandoned my daughter on the side of the road…or kill her on our way here.

My shoulders burned, but I tugged against my hog-tied bindings. I caught a glimpse of Tula's charcoal sleeve peeking over the side of the wagon bed.

She wasn't moving. My gut knotted.

A hand cracked across my rump, and I jolted from the sharp sting. Sibley leaned over my back to get closer to my ear. "We're here, Henry. Time ta give yer pound of flesh," he taunted with a chuckle. "Judge Mathis'll have a ball with you. Ain't no one in Savannah gonna protest on yer behalf, neither. Can't have a known killer goin' 'round thinkin' they have the upper hand 'round here, now, can we?"

"Why? Are you all afraid I'll make you look like the weak bunch of pigs you are?" I asked, my tone laced with false saccharine.

Sibley didn't reply. He shifted in the saddle and climbed down off his horse. His black leather boots sunk into the mud just below my head. Another pair of light brown boots, scuffed and worn to the point of holes appearing at the toes, stepped beside him.

"She a mouthy one, ain't she?" Sibley's associate mumbled above me. He moved closer, the unimpressive bulge under his front flap nudged the crown of my head. "I got sumtin' ta stuff dat purdy mouf wit'."

The reek of days-old sweat and ass-rot wafted into my nostrils, and I grimaced. In one swift motion, I jerked my head up, slamming my skull into his groin.

He doubled, cradling his goods in two quivering hands. Slowly, he stumbled away from me. Once he found his breath again, he let out a wounded groan and a smattering of words so foul they'd make the raunchiest woman blush.

I grinned, appeased by the mongrel's swaying charade of agony.

He released a shuttering breath then straightened on wobbly legs. His expression morphed from wounded to vengeful. His eyes flared with rage. In three hasty strides, he closed in on me, locked my head between his dirty palms, and threw his knee up into my face.

My nose crunched. The intense barb of pain shot through my brain like a glowing fire-poker. Tears gathered in my eyes. The world spun. My vision glazed over. If I weren't tied to a horse, I would've toppled over.

The taste of a tangy penny oozed onto my tongue, accompanied by warm liquid draining from my sinuses. I coughed, spitting a mouthful of blood onto the horse's shiny hide.

He crouched down next to my ear, huffing. "Dat shoul' shut yer feisty yap fer a while."

The dizziness making a merry-go-round of my perception evened, but I couldn't shake away the little drummer boy beating an infuriating rhythm inside my skull. I stared beyond the horse's underbelly at a clump of rust-colored muck sludging down a spoke on the wagon wheel and tried to gain my wits.

"I'll have my stable boy return this wagon to you in the mornin', Sibley," Deveraux said.

"Fine, fine," Sibley agreed. "I'm sure yer eager to get the girl home. From the looks, it'll take some days ta get 'er accustomed to 'er new rules. She seems quite the mule when it come ta followin' directions."

Sibley tramped behind his horse and approached my legs. Ropes bit into my abraded wrists and ankles as he loosened the knots. "I'm sure Judge Mathis'll wanna hear from ya, ta get yer side of the story an' all." Sibley rested his forearm on the crest of my behind, speaking over me with the same concern he'd grant his saddle. "Shouldn't be anythin' too cumbersome, though. She's dug quite a deep grave all by 'erself."

"Let my boy know when the judge would prefer my presence," Deveraux replied. Leather snapped, and the wagon rocked forward.

I jerked, a lump of panic clogging my throat. He was leaving...with Tula. Flailing my body, I fought against the remaining tethers holding me in place.

"Emil, grab 'er arms, dammit," Sibley grunted, wrestling with my scissoring legs.

The horse canted left, butting into Sibley. He hugged my calves, using my lower half to keep himself upright, despite the large skittish animal shoving into him.

I wriggled my hands free of the bindings and reached for the saddle horn, but Emil grabbed my wrists before I found leverage to right myself.

Deveraux snapped his reins again, driving Millie to trudge forward.

"Tula," I screamed, punching the air between Emil and me to break free of his grip.

Her still form sprang to life, squirming in the back of the wagon. A shrill cry let me know she heard me.

"I'll find you," I rasped. "I promise."

"Don't make vows ya can't keep," Emil advised. He released one of my hands, pulled back his elbow, then thrust his fist toward me.

I blinked rapidly, sucking in a surprised breath. The blow was too fast—too hard. My cheekbone lit on fire.

Swirling specks of light danced across my vision. I pressed my eyelids together then opened them wide, trying to focus beyond the specks.

Silas's wagon turned right out of the courthouse's driveway.

Tula was gone.

My body went limp over the horse's spine, and my vision flickered out like an extinguished flame.

It seemed like only seconds, but the next time I opened my eyes, everything had changed. Someone untied me from the horse and carried me inside the courthouse.

I lay on a stone floor, my swollen, aching cheek planted in a pool of yellow fluid. I winced and inhaled sharply, shocked by the pain spreading through my face. The acrid odor of piss and shit hit me so hard, I tasted it.

Scrambling up on my knees, I scrubbed the waste from my face with my torn sleeve. My eyes roved over the cramped cell imprisoning me. Thick chains hung from shackles fixed in the stone walls, traces of dried blood caked on the dull metal. A cracked porcelain chamber pot rested on a bed of decomposing hay in the far corner.

I swiped the back of my hand over my nose. The odor was so foul it embedded in my nostrils. A mouse traipsed around broken pieces of brick on the floor. There was no use trying to avoid the cell's unpleasantries; it wouldn't get any better than this. I pressed myself into the cold wall behind me and frowned.

"Welcome, Ms. James," a rich voice greeted me.

I twisted, scanning the dimly lit hall just outside my cage.

An older gentleman, in his late sixties maybe, leaned forward in a chair resting against the wall opposite my cell.

"I'm Sheriff Cunningham." He peered through the bars penning me in this dank, rot-infested room. His gaze was scrutinizing beneath his topper brim. "I've heard quite the story about you. Care to give me your side?"

The sheriff's unreadable expression was almost calming. It was a nice alternative to the ugly, judgmental sneers directed toward me by his men and Mr. Deveraux. From the crinkles around his eyes and the distinctive laugh lines framing his thin lips, I gathered he was a kinder person than those ruthless heathens, one who enjoyed humor and happiness. And he was the only one who asked to hear my version of the accusations.

Perhaps he really did want to hear my story. Maybe there was a chance he'd have pity on me and bestow understanding on my tragic tale.

Or, his sincerity could be a scheme to hear my confession and hang me from the scaffolds sooner than later.

I sealed my lips tight. He couldn't use my words to incriminate me if I kept silent. In the end, Judge Mathis would make his decision based on his position in office and the statements of his peers, especially those filling his pockets, not any explanation I gave.

"I see," he said, settling back into his chair and crossing an ankle on his knee. His steady hand straightened the creased lapel of his long jacket, then he brushed lint from his pant leg. Polished brass buttons and a stately star pinned to his right chest gleamed under the gas lamp above his head. "All I have to go by is the claims brought against you by Mr. Deveraux and Mr. Pike. There's no need to investigate any further, since you refuse to give a statement, Ms. James. You're as good as dead, if you don't speak up." His stern eyes rose to meet mine, a trace of compassion softening his gaze. "You have nothing to say for yourself?"

I pushed myself up off the dirty floor and shuffled toward him like an old woman, my aching muscles protesting the movement. Fisting an iron bar in each hand, I said, "I'm as good as dead if I do speak, so what difference will it make?"

We stared each other down in a moment of silence, assessing if we were friends or foes.

"Did you murder Mr. Shamus Kingly?"

I bit my tongue, denying him my confession.

He sighed. "Did you attempt to poison Mr. Edison Pike?"

Dropping my hands, I turned away and wandered to the small window carved out of a large stone near the ceiling. Rain continued to fall, and gray strings of clouds blotted out the radiant moon.

"Ms. James? Holding your tongue will only make them think you're guilty."

"Sheriff Cunningham, it doesn't matter whether I'm guilty or not. It doesn't matter what reasons brought me to this point in my life," I deadpanned, frowning up at the sliver of silver moon. "I probably belong in here. So, go ahead, believe what they've told you," I spun to face him, crossing my arms over my growling stomach, "but I'm tellin' you now, they better hope I never make it out of here."

He pinched one side of the mustache winging out from his top lip, twisting it between his fingertips. He observed me, contemplating my sincerity. "I'd be careful not to make threats that might incriminate you further, Ms."

Rising from the chair with the ease and confidence of a man in complete control of every matter of his life, he approached our barrier. He rested his wrist on the butt of the pistol fastened to his hip and licked his lips. "There's suspicions of Mr. Deveraux and some of his business associates engaging in criminal acts. Would you know anything about that, Ms. James?" Pacing the bars, he waited patiently for me to answer.

I shook my head.

I didn't have any proof Mr. Deveraux raped and shot Tula's mother. They wouldn't believe Tula's testimony either. The judge would certainly take his word over mine.

He slowed, leaning his back against the wall adjacent to my cell. He plucked a pipe from his jacket pocket. Lighting the bowl, he inhaled several quick puffs then let the smoke float from his mouth. Staring at the white haze, he said, "There are two kinds of men in Savannah. Those who have worked hard, abided rules, sought peace, and learned to respect the folks around him, no matter color or gender." He picked a dried speck of tobacco leaf from the stem of his pipe and flicked it from his thumb. "And there are those who insist on impeding their ignorant, closed-minded ideals on the rest for the sake of power and gain. They like to bully the good-doers of our town, using fear and misfortune to drive people into doing their bidding."

His steely gaze drifted to the side, peeking at me from under the deep brim of his hat. "Those men really throw a wrench in my cogs."

Strong jaw muscles churned under the white stubble on his cheeks. "I'd like to keep Savannah a tidy place, where folks are proud to live and enjoy visiting, but I can't do that when greasy villains slip out of my grasp so easily. I've tried to build a case against Deveraux and his allies for some time now, and I can't seem to get past the pristine business records to get to the dirt. Even his workers won't help me." He looked at his smoldering tobacco thoughtfully. "I'm not sure what he's done to convince them to keep silent, but they're too afraid to speak ill about the man in the least."

I knew how Deveraux worked. He was using the same tactics on me. He found what mattered most and stole it or threatened to defile it until you caved, giving into whatever he required of you. It was such a simple thing, but effective.

Peering down at my crossed forearms, I mulled over telling the sheriff what I knew.

He whistled a tune of disappointment, wandering back to his chair. Sheriff Cunningham sat down, exhaling loudly. "I was really hoping you'd help me out, Ms. James. I hate to see ladies suffer at Judge Mathis's dirty hands...especially those who were just trying to preserve themselves from ill fates." He sunk back against the backrest and dipped his head down, tugging his hat over his brow.

Backing into a corner, I crouched on the floor with my soiled skirts tucked close around me. My scattered thoughts were a loud backdrop, mingling among the possibilities of what would happen to me, Tula, and Silas.

I spent the rest of the night watching the horrid morning approach, listening to Cunningham's throaty snores, and wondering if I'd die the next day.

Chapter Eighteen

Silas

I slid off Domino, not bothering to tie him to the post. Bounding up Edison's steps, I ignored the pain shooting up my thigh and pounded on his door.

"Pike," I shouted, beating the wood with my fist so hard my wrist ached. "Open the fucking door, you coward."

I flattened my ear against the wood. Wind rustling through the pear tree in his front yard, rain pelting his worn steps, and my labored breathing created quite the racquet outside, but there wasn't a single sound coming from inside.

"Pike," I roared again. Lightening crackled, drenching everything in a white glow then submerging me in darkness quicker than the thump of my heart. Stepping back, I searched the second-floor windows. A dim light pulsed through one of the panes.

Thunder rolled, provoking Pike's horses to whine from the stable to my left. He was here, but true to his character, he was lying in wait until someone else did his dirty work.

Gnashing my teeth, I bolted for the door, slamming into the hard surface. The jamb splintered, and the brass lock plate gave. I tumbled inside, rubbing my throbbing shoulder. "Edison, I know you're here."

Taking two steps at a time, I raced to the room where I saw the light—the same room I found Synthia and Tula in before.

I turned the corner to enter, then came to an abrupt stop.

Clack.

Pike met me at the door, a revolver aimed between my brows, cocked and ready to fire. "What were you sayin', Mr. Burke?"

I shifted my jaw, chewing on the slurs I wanted to blurt out. Stiffening my spine, I stood tall, waiting for him to pull the trigger.

A slow laugh rumbled from his belly, his eyes sparkling with the satisfaction of victory. "I bet you thought you had me good at the meeting. Did you think I was just gonna sit back and let you dictate my affairs for me? I don't know who you are, Silas, but I think you've gotten yourself knee-deep in your own shit." He jabbed the muzzle into the narrow space separating us. "I've worked too damn hard, made too many sacrifices, for a bootlicker like you to mosey in and steal my claim to fortune."

"Sacrifices? Let's speak of those sacrifices, then. What have you forgone to become such a fancy man?"

His smile faded, his upper lip curling into a sneer.

"You've only made it as far as you have by stepping on other people's backs…just like the men you are in cahoots with. You'll never be an honorable man. I don't know how you can live with yourself, really," I spat.

Edison's nostrils flared. A glint of shame mixed with fiery anger darkened his eyes. He eased forward, pressing cold metal to my forehead.

"She'll never be happy with you," he said, switching the subject to something he knew would niggle at my own weaknesses. "Synthia's too wild to be tamed by your sort. She needs a dominant hand to force her into line. You don't have it in you to be the fellow she needs." His mouth quirked up when my shoulders broadened and my lips cinched into a tight line. He ruffled me, and he knew it. "She always comes back to me in the end."

"She comes back to you because you leave her with nothing. You take every bit of dignity and goodness in her heart, trampling it until it's confused and insecure. You're ruining her, don't you see that?" Edison's iron gaze bore into mine, unaffected by my charges. "You don't even care, do you?"

Before he spouted anymore ridiculous reasons for his greatness, I retaliated. I shot my hands upward, bringing my palms together in a strong bracket, and thrusted the gun's barrel toward the ceiling.

Bang.

Pike fired an errant bullet into the unlit gas sconce over my right shoulder. Pungent gun smoke invaded my nose. Glass clattered to the floor, and a sharp ring from the blast resonated in my ears.

Gripping the hot metal, I jerked the pistol back and forth, trying to snatch it from Pike's determined hands before he blew a hole into me instead of the house.

Spittle flew from Edison's gritted teeth, dotting my face as we battled for power over the weapon. We shuffled farther into the room, twisting this way and that until his legs bumped into his bed.

Struggling to stay upright, Edison bowed backwards against my force. His grip on the gun was weakening, and I almost wrenched it from his fingers.

"She will forget about you…when you're gone, Burke. She'll soon remember…who cares for her…who's taken care of her all these years. In a few days, I'll pay the judge off and get her out. I'm sure Synthia will run right back into…my arms," he rasped. He fell onto the edge of his mattress then slumped to the floor.

I toppled with him, my hands assuming possession of the wooden grip. "In a few days, she might be dead."

Edison groaned, scurrying on top of me in a panic to gain control over the weapon once again. He hooked his thumb in the trigger guard. "She. Is. Mine," he roared.

The gun bucked in our hands, an unforgiving bullet basting from the barrel between us. The shot echoed through the room, rendering me deaf for a short time.

Our eyes widened, beaming at each other in surprise. Warm liquid pulled on my chest, and I waited for the burning agony of another gunshot wound. I held my breath, expecting my heartbeat to slow and my lungs to give out.

It never came.

Edison's mouth opened, blood burbling up with his words. "She… is…mi…" His eyes glazed over, heavy lids sealing them shut for the final time.

The restrained weight of his body relaxed, and he collapsed onto my torso. He felt twice as heavy now that he was dead.

I lay on Edison's floor, peering up at a spidery crack in the ceiling, allowing my heart to steady. A dull thwap to my right caused another startling jolt in my chest. Jerking my head towards the sound, I noticed a journal hidden under the shadows of Edison's bed. Strings of frayed mattress hung above the leather-bound pages. It must've wiggled its way through the springs during our fight.

Pushing Edison's stiff shoulders, I rolled him to the side and inhaled a lungful of air. I shimmied my legs out from under his dead-weight and slid closer to the bed, eyeing the thick, worn book. Reaching a blood-smeared hand under the bed, I retrieved the object.

I sat up, holding the journal in my palm. I flipped through the pages slowly, scanning over every selfish, conniving word.

He'd documented every day for the past several years, laying out his emotions for Synthia after his wife and child died and his greedy plans for their future. He went into specifics about their informal fostering of Tula and the day he found out Deveraux was looking for her because she witnessed the brutal treatment and death of her mother by his hand.

He weaseled his way into Deveraux's group by collecting witnesses and pieces of evidence which could prove their most heinous criminal acts over the years. Edison used the proof to manipulate their tolerance and gain invitation into their ranks. He was craftier than I believed him to be.

He accounted the murder he'd pushed on Synthia, blackmailing her with Tula. He wrote of his plans to have her kill me, along with a Mr. Burlington who had yet to arrive in Savannah.

This was his insurance in life, a ledger safeguarding each small step he made toward prosperity.

It was Edison's downfall too.

It was a collection of damning pages that could free my love.

A grin pulled at my lips. I glanced over at Edison's corpse. "Thanks for being such a wonderful scribe, you despicable sack of horseshit. This should undo the hell you've created," I said, shaking the journal at him. "Now, what am I gonna do with you?"

Pushing to my feet, I dragged the dingy-white sheet from the mattress. I almost felt sorry for the man spread out in a motionless heap at my boots. He could've had so much more if he'd only treated her with respect. He could've found the world in her arms.

I understood what he would miss because I vowed to wrap myself in her bosom, surrender every part of my life to her, give her everything I had. I'd make certain all my days were filled with her dark, earthy scent, her loving embraces, and her passionate love.

I flattened the sheet along Edison's side and began rolling him into the linen. Blood seeped through the thin threads, reminding me of the night I watched Synthia at the swamp, and I realized the perfect way to dispose of his body.

Chapter Nineteen

The dawning sun leeched into the picture-sized window above my head. A ray of warmth cascaded across my shaking hands, warming my icy fingers as I picked at my skirt. I twisted and scratched at the brown threads so mindlessly throughout the night, the fibers between my fingers tore, creating a tiny hole as if a moth fed on it.

At some point, I'd left my chilly perch nestled in the corner to traverse the filthy cell. I had gathered my dress around my thighs and hovered over the chamber pot, relieving myself. The simple, natural enactment caused another shred of dignity to leave my body in a steady flow along with the piss filling the cracked porcelain.

Sheriff Cunningham's eyes were closed during the humiliating act, but I suspected he'd roused when his snoring ceased at the first sounds of my movement.

Afterwards, I returned to my corner, far from the waste area, and huddled back into my tight ball of despair. I'd sifted through all the ways I might be able to elude him and escape my cell. With little I could use for weaponry at my disposal, I didn't have any luck advancing my plans.

The sheriff stayed cemented to the same chair all night, never once leaving to eat or relieve his own bladder. He seemed to have iron will when it came to his natural needs. Since he was always there to witness my every move, my efforts of scouring the cell for weak points were limited.

I'd settled on the strategy of waiting until he opened the door to retrieve me then fight with all my might and hope I broke free of his hold long enough to run like hell. I still had my boot heels; I could stomp his toes. Perhaps, I could disable him even more by slamming the chipped piece of brick I'd hidden in my bodice against his temple or in his eye. It would work far more efficiently than my fist.

Whatever it took for me to get to Tula, I'd do it with no regrets.

The clack of heavy boots echoed down the hall. I stiffened, snapping my attention toward the sound. Sheriff Cunningham's eyes popped open. He shot out of his chair, his bushy brow furrowing with distrust then relaxing the smallest fraction when he saw who entered the building.

With a slight tip of his hat, he greeted the newcomer through tight lips. "Judge Mathis."

A portly figure wobbled in from the hallway shadows. The dim light sheened off his overly greased, thinning hair and sweaty forehead. Judge Mathis snagged a handkerchief from his coat pocket and wiped it over the pronounced wrinkles rippling above his brow.

He was a well-fed older man. Based on the permanent sour expression imprinted on his pug-like face, he didn't appear to have a lick of compassion running in his veins.

"For the love of God, I cannot fathom why you insist on having the prisoners stored down here, Cunningham," he huffed in a gruff,

Southern drawl. He swiped his dampened kerchief over his face one more time then stuffed the yellowing cloth back in his pocket. "I ought to have *you* arrested for making me travel down so many damn steps."

Sheriff Cunningham pursed his lips at the bitter comment and waited for the judge to finish catching his breath.

I eased up the wall, keeping my back pressed against the cold stone, and studied the disquiet rolling between the two men.

Judge Mathis noticed my movement and turned his irritated gaze toward me. A spark of intrigue lit his black eyes.

"So," he mused, framing his potbelly between meaty fingers like it was his most handsome feature, "this is our Ms. James." His eyes glittered, roaming over my body the same way I'd imagined he might if I were a prized ham. Flecks of intrigue and triumph mingled among the dark prospects reflecting in his irises.

He tottered his short legs in my direction, curving his fat, dry mouth in a nasty smile. "I've heard so much about you." Leaning his face inches from the door, he angled his left eye between two bars to see me better. "Don't worry, your misery will be over quickly. Hanging is the most efficient way to go."

Images of my hometown hanging a thief when I was a girl flashed in my mind. It wasn't quick. He jerked for what felt like hours, though it wasn't. The thief bit clean through his tongue. Blood poured from his mouth and he seized at the end of the line for a long time before finally asphyxiating.

I knew better than to be thankful for the ending Judge Mathis was planning for me and my misery.

The sheriff stepped forward, his square jaw hardened, and gripped Judge Mathis's upper arm. "I believe she deserves a trial, Judge."

Whipping his pudgy body around, Judge Mathis scowled up at Sheriff Cunningham in disbelief. "You do, do you?" He yanked his arm from Cunningham's hand. "I don't *believe* it much matters. This woman," he spat the word as if he thought "demon" would be a better title for me, "murdered one of our most promising investors. Murder is punishable by death, Sheriff. An eye for an eye and all that. It seems cut and dry to me. The reasonable people of Savannah won't see it any other way, I'm sure. No need to prolong the inevitable with a silly trial."

"But she has the right to explain her reasonings. She could have a fair purpose for harming her victims, Judge." The sheriff's eyes flicked to me. Concern underlined his stern expression. "Will you not give her the same chance you gave the man we arrested two months ago? He was allowed a trial after beating his child to death for disobedience."

Judge Mathis puckered his mouth, glaring at me over his shoulder with a moment's consideration. He faced the sheriff again. "I've spoken to Mr. Deveraux, and I don't think we can afford the time or efforts it would take to allow such a privilege."

"*We*?" Cunningham probed. He shook his head. "You mean the town can't afford it?" His wise eyes narrowed at the judge. "Or, do you mean *you* can't afford what it would do to your reputation and the men feeding your hefty pockets?"

Judge Mathis's mulish expression faltered for a breath, then he tipped up his nose and replaced his obstinate mask. "It's not your place to question my decision in matters like these, Thomas." He nodded his head curtly, settled on his final thought. "Gather the girl. Let's get this over with." He whirled on his heels, waddling toward the stairs.

Sheriff Cunningham dropped his head, resting his hands on his hips. He was trying to work in my favor to the best of his abilities, without betraying his duties. It was plain in the pity washing over his face when he realized Mathis wouldn't budge.

Steeling his composure, he marched toward me. He pulled a ring of keys from his back pocket and inserted one into my cell lock. "Come on, Ms. James. You heard the man." The hint of a silent apology lingered behind his stoic gaze.

Once he swung open the door, I pushed back my shoulders and lifted my chin. He was only doing what was right. I was a criminal and should be punished for my sins. There was no reason for me to cower from justice.

I brushed back the short, oily curls flattened against my forehead and took a deep, resolute breath. Stepping forward, I held out my wrists, preparing for the shackles awaiting me.

He latched one cuff around my arm then stilled. His head shot to the left where Judge Mathis's boots skidded to a stop.

"You don't belong down here, son," the judge scorned from the dark stairwell.

A voice I longed to hear bounced off the brick walls. "I have business to address on behalf of Ms. Synthia James."

My heart stuttered, and I held back a sob of relief.

Silas was alive.

Sheriff Cunningham swiftly turned his back to me, placing himself between me and Silas. He thrust back one flap of his jacket and rested his right hand on the butt of his gun, gauging the threat of Silas's interaction with Judge Mathis.

"Ms. James's business is none of yours," the judge barked.

Silas limped forward. I saw a glimpse of his handsome face in the low light. Dark half-moons rimmed his lower eyelids. The shadows exaggerated a bruise forming above the bridge of his nose. His clean clothes were a stark contrast to his marred and beaten body. He looked like he'd been through hell to get here, and the gloss of desperation in his eyes only confirmed it.

Silas slapped something against Judge Mathis's chest. "She *is* my business, sir. I'm bringing you proof she was coerced to commit criminal acts under duress at the hand of Mr. Edison Pike."

The judge smacked his lips together, glancing over his shoulder at me and Cunningham with a doubtful expression. Focusing back on Silas, he said, "I don't know what you're getting at here, young man, but I hardly think a book will have enough useful information to pardon this woman of her crimes." He shoved the book back at Silas, not bothering to skim over even one word inside.

My lover thrust his hand out, shoving the book back at the judge. "Your honor, please. Read Edison's journal. It's obvious he manipulated her into what she's accused of," he pleaded.

Sheriff Cunningham twisted toward me, searching my face. "Is this true?" he asked softly.

Judge Mathis chortled. "How am I to know you didn't write these yourself?" He turned partly to address Cunningham. "They warned me about this man, Thomas. He's in band with this one." He flung his hand in my direction. "Without Mr. Pike here to speak for himself, I cannot give this any consideration."

The sheriff advanced toward the judge. "Now, hold on, Mathis. You are ready to hang this woman without a trial based on what some rather shady men have implied. Yet, you won't take a moment to read a journal that might pardon Ms. James of some very serious crimes simply because the author is not here to defend himself?"

While the two men debated, Silas's gaze met mine. He winked, discretely tapping a finger at his hip. The motion hinted at a hard object secured under his coat. The outline was similar to Cunningham's gun when hidden under his jacket.

I nodded. He was not going to let them take me easily.

Judge Mathis lowered his head, sneering. "I cannot entertain this nonsense any longer," he argued. Squaring his shoulders, he continued, "I've stated my sentence. Now, if you care about your job, Sheriff, you'll do as I say and ready the criminal."

Cunningham stayed frozen to his spot, his fists clenched at his side.

The judge cleared his throat and tugged his belt up over his robust belly. "I'll see you upstairs when you are finished here. Jacob will summon the executioner and have him hang the noose."

Judge Mathis turned, and Silas smacked the butt of his pistol against his temple. The judge teetered, looking dazed for a moment, then collapsed to the ground.

Cunningham gasped. His hand bolted for the gun on his right hip but came up empty. Patting the vacant holster, he spun to face me. His eyes widened. The weapon he'd meant to retrieve seconds before was firmly encased in my small hands and pointed at the center of his forehead.

"Sorry, Sheriff, but I don't plan on hanging until I make sure my affairs are settled." I edged around him in a slow circle.

Silas rushed to my side, patting the sheriff down until he found the ring of keys in his pocket. I kept my aim with one hand while my love unlocked the shackle from my other wrist. The hunk of metal clanked to the floor, and I smiled. "I'm sure I will atone for my crimes soon enough, sir, but for now, I'll be doing what I promised you."

I took Edison's journal from Silas's hand and slung it into Cunningham's chest. The shock of me stealing his weapon and Silas beating the judge drained from his face. He held the book over his heart, a spark of curiosity and hope igniting in his eyes.

"Maybe this will help you find a way to impart the justice you've sought." I trusted his intentions and his judgement for some reason. His protest on my behalf told me he wasn't a man who did things for the wrong reasons. I hoped he'd put whatever was in Edison's journal to good use.

I stepped forward. The sheriff stepped back. Despite the fact we both knew he could easily disarm me, he allowed me to control the situation. I steered him backward until he was inside the cell then closed the bars between us. Lowering the gun, I studied his stoic expression. "You better move fast, though, Sheriff Cunningham. I'd hate to see something happen to those men before you were able to punish them lawfully."

He leaned closer to me, hanging a hand from one of the bars. "Don't do anything to make your ending harder, Ms. James."

"My life has been nothing but hard, Sheriff, so why would I expect any different."

"Come on, Synthia," Silas urged, touching a gentle hand to my shoulder. "He's waking."

I glanced at the judge sprawled on the floor like a starfish. He rolled his head lazily from side to side and groaned.

Gripping the same bar Cunningham held on to, I stared him in the eyes. His impervious expression softened, and he smiled.

"Happy reading." Perhaps I could trust him after all.

Silas laced my fingers in his and pulled. I followed him out of the prison, leaving my execution for another day.

Chapter Twenty

Silas hoisted me up by the waist, practically throwing me onto Domino. I scooted into place and shuffled my skirt around my knees, so I could ride astride for a better grip.

Shoving his boot into the stirrup, my love climbed atop his obsidian horse and settled in front of me. He wound his hands in the reins and blew out a sharp, ear-piercing whistle. Domino jolted into action. The steed ran full speed, putting miles between us and the men who would soon be after us.

I held tight to Silas's waist. "Where's Edison?"

"You won't have to worry about him ever again," he tossed over his shoulder.

"What did you say to make him leave?"

Silas didn't respond, but one of his hands smoothed over the fingers I'd clasped at his heart, telling me he heard me. He just wasn't willing to answer.

"He'll come back, Silas. He won't leave me with you," I shouted, a rumble of distant thunder adding a sinister backdrop to my words. The rain passed, but the ground was drenched. Moisture clung to the air with the storm still brewing only a few miles from us.

"I'm only worried about getting you somewhere dry and safe at the moment."

A flicker of lightening illuminated a shortcut in the woods I knew led to the back side of the swamp behind my home. I scraped my teeth over my bottom lip, letting the subject fade.

"There." I pointed East.

Silas shook his head. "No. This is too close to the courthouse and Pike's home."

I curled my fingers around his forearm and gently tugged, urging his hand to draw the reins toward the right. "I know what I'm doing. Please, just take that path."

Soft droplets of rain tapped our shoulders. Silas looked up at the onset of new rain. He growled and turned Domino into the wood line.

We trotted along the worn trail until we met the edge of my swamp. Before the horse stopped completely, I slid down, my boots sinking in the softened earth.

"Woah," Silas called out. "What are you doing?"

Peering up at him, I pointed toward the small island of solid ground I knew was hidden beyond the dense veil of water-logged Cypresses and tree hair. "Through there."

Silas squinted at the swamp, unable to see where I proposed we hide. Canting his head to the side, he perched a fist on his hip and draped his other arm atop the saddle horn. "Through where?" he questioned skeptically.

"Through the water." I jutted my chin at the expanse of motionless algae-green film blanketing the run-off from Ogeechee River.

Silas shifted in his saddle, the leather creaking under his movement. He folded his arms over his chest and stared down at me as if I'd grown a tail.

I threw my hands out to my sides. "What?"

I imagined anybody searching for us would have the same reaction and wouldn't dare cross the stagnant water to hunt us down. But, really, it was just water. I had crossed it a thousand times. Rarely, did I run into a gator threatened enough to bother with me. It was usually the water moccasins I worried about.

"No, ma'am. You can't swim that," he protested, slipping off Domino.

I trudged forward, gathering my dress in my arms and clumsily taking off my boots as I walked. "I assure you, Mr. Burke, I can. Did you forget, you've seen me wading the swamp in the past?" I glanced over my shoulder where Silas stood planted to his spot beside Domino. A worry-crease crinkled his forehead, reluctance warring with his need to follow me anywhere.

"There's a million other places to hide, Synthia," he whined. "Can't you come up with a less…gator-riddled location?"

Shaking my head, I dipped my toes into the mushy shore. I inhaled sharply, the cooler water contrasting with the somewhat warm autumn climate. Another reason the cowards wouldn't venture into the swamp after me. "This is the only place I can be truly safe, Silas."

Throwing the bulk of my skirt over my arm, I inhaled and held my boots high above my head to keep them dry, then move forward.

He gripped my elbow, bringing me to a stop. "I have a friend three towns over. I'm sure his family would welcome you. I can come back for Tula."

I turned, willing him to see the certainty in my eyes. "I will not leave here without her. She is mine, and I refuse to allow that man to have her a second longer than necessary. I'm going to cross this damned swamp, hide out for the night, and devise a way to get her back. By noon tomorrow, I will have my daughter…with or without you." Casting my gaze over the wet forest to avoid his piercing eyes, I whispered, "I love you, Silas, but she will always be the center of my world."

He raised his hands up in surrender, swearing under his breath. Mumbling, he stomped back to his horse.

My heart splintered, watching him give-up on me so easily, but maybe it was for the best. I clopped into the limey water's edge, expelling a squeak of discomfort as I adjusted to the temperature.

Seconds later, a disturbance in the water behind me lapped against my thighs and a loud hiss of breath perked my ears.

Silas groaned. "Christ, it's fucking frigid in here, woman."

I stopped, eyeing him from a few paces ahead. My bottom lip was starting to tremble from the chill. Soon, my skin would look like a plucked goose. The warm weather made the water feel colder than it really was, and it was harder to acclimate to. Smiling at Silas sloshing toward me, I said, "Deep breaths. It'll help calm your system 'til you adjust."

He stumbled into a soft spot below the water's surface and fell to one knee. Water splashed up around his chest. A deluge of curses flew from his snarling lips.

Without meaning to, I giggled. He was so flustered, it was too entertaining not to react.

Silas lifted his narrowed gaze from the green water inches from his chin and glared at me. He pulled a dripping arm up and smacked the murky river.

A wave of wet scum slung toward me, sprinkling my shoulders and neck. I closed my eyes, gasping from the shock of cold pelting my warm upper body.

The swamp sloshed again, ripples of Silas's movements breaking against my thighs. When I opened my eyes, his grinning face was so close to mine I could tilt my chin up and kiss him.

He wrapped his arms around me, whispering, "Don't worry, you get me out of this swamp before I die of hypothermia, I promise to warm you back up." His bluing lips brushed my brow, my nose, then settled a soft kiss on my quivering mouth.

The rough spines of gator-skin scraped my ankle, but I stayed calm. It was not the first time I'd felt the reptiles explore me. I'd worked hard to make them understand I wasn't a threat during my visits, and I learned not to panic. If I alerted Silas, though, he would most certainly panic.

"Let's go then," I whispered back. Taking his hand, I turned slowly for my destination. We waded through the water slowly, cautious of what was beneath our feet.

I noted the s-shaped wakes undulating along the tree trunks and steered us away from the moccasins in the area. Only two sets of reflective eyes breached the algae-blanket to spy on us, but they swam away, keeping their distance.

Twenty minutes into our journey, the soil began to slope upward. We slowed, catching sight of the small wooden shack sitting curiously in the center of the only dry island in the entirety of Edison's swamp.

Silas's brow rose, appraising the cracked boards and eroded clay mortar holding the structure upright. "How long has this been here?"

I shrugged a shoulder. "Not sure. I found it the first time I ran from Edison. He wanted Tula to seduce an upstate farmer with a penchant for young women and steal the plant combinations he used to make his crops so unique. When she refused, he locked her in the cellar without food. I eventually did what he asked in her place, hoping he'd let her out. It worked. He released her from the cellar after I got the information, but he realized what power he had over me. That night, I came out here. I thought, if I wasn't in the picture, he wouldn't be able to use her against me.

"I was determined to let the alligators have me for dinner. I trudged through the swamp for hours, waiting for them to attack, but they never did. The rest of my evening was spent sobbing on that floor." I ticked my head toward the moss-adorned building. "I gathered all the pain he caused me and shoved it down." I balled my fist over the base of my stomach. "When I was dry as ash, I vowed I wouldn't leave Tula alone to deal with his cruel ways by herself ever again. I realized he would use her as his pawn whether I was there or not." Plodding forward, I shivered, a breeze slithering around my wet knees. "Edison is resourceful, which you've seen, and he has little qualms about doing whatever it takes to get what he wants. He would've hunted me to the ends of the Earth. So, I went back."

Silas tramped up the marshy ground beside me. "How many times did you leave him, Synthia?"

Pondering the short spans of disillusioned courage I'd gained over the past years, I stepped out of the water fully and tossed my boots on a wet patch of grass. I wrung my dripping dress. Images of Tula and I flagging a cargo wagon on its way to Texas, then Edison dragging us out of the back miles down the road, flashed through my mind. Memories of pinching money from his wallet without his notice for months to board a ship departing for the Caribbean, only to have him waiting on the dock when we got there soured my stomach. There were one or two more times we tried to flee his control, but he was always a step ahead of us.

Letting my skirt fall to the ground, I turned to face Silas. "There were many times. He always thwarted our attempts. Eventually, we gave up." I picked up my boots and held them upside down, dumping out the water that had splashed between the laces. "Perhaps, it was for the best...who knows what would have happened to two women traveling on their own. It was fear of an unknown future, and fear of Edison's retaliation, chaining us to him so strongly."

Silas dropped his pack off his shoulder and wound his arm to release the tension there. He held out his hand to me. "Are you still afraid?"

"No," I affirmed, shaking my head. "I'm pissed. There's no room in me for fright or apprehension anymore. Only revenge and grit." I took his hand, my heart swelling from the proud smile curving his lips.

He pointed his thumb toward the cabin. "Come on, let's get warm."

Chapter Twenty-One

We trekked up the shallow hill raising the shack out of the swamp's reach. Silas occasionally bent down, collecting random branches and kindling on his way to the front porch.

While he inspected the area, I ventured to the rear of the cabin. There was a shallow well out back I had discovered it during one of my earlier nights on the island.

Staring down into the black, yawning pit, I prayed there was still fresh water in it. I pulled a tattered rope swaying from a crossbeam above the well, feeling something heavy swinging at the end. Hopefully, it still had a useable bucket attached, not one with holes rotted in it from the constant moisture. When I found the end of the line, a sizable wooden pail popped over the stone ledge. Fresh water spilled over the edge.

Cupping my hands, I scooped a bit of water into my palms and sipped the cool, clean liquid. I hummed in appreciation, savoring the wetness coating my cotton-dry mouth. I removed the lids on our empty canteens and dunked them into the pail, filling each one to the brim.

I quickly tossed the bucket back into the well then tugged it up again. Bending over, I dipped the top of my head into the water. I scrubbed my hands through my grimy hair then used what was left to clean the other important bits of my body. Being somewhat clean felt wonderful after not bathing in two days.

I slicked my hands through my dripping auburn curls one more time then returned the bucket to the dark bottom of the well. Roaming back to Silas, I gathered my own pile of kindling.

I came around the side of the cabin, joining Silas on the porch. His hands were framed around his eyes, searching the broken windows for signs of life inside.

"Anyone home?" I asked.

He backed away from the window and shook his head. "Not that I can see."

Smiling, I scanned the front of the old house and reveled in the sense of familiarity. It felt like coming home. It was where I came to hide when things were at their worst with Edison. It was my sanctuary. "Didn't figure there would be."

Once he was sure the property was vacant, he shoved his hip into the door. Rusty hinges only allowed the rectangle of narrow planks to open halfway, but it was enough for us to squeeze through.

I leaned back against the door, forcing it closed behind us with a loud squeal form the straining hinges.

Silas chuckled. "At least we'll know if anyone tries to enter." He slung his pack on the floor, inspecting the single room surrounding us.

My eyes followed his, cataloguing the limited furnishings I was already acquainted with. There was a small box stove sitting in the corner, with a large black smoke stain marking the ceiling just above it. Against the far wall was a table laden with dust so thick it looked as though there was a gray cloth covering its bare frame.

Our gazes dropped at the same time, noticing the pile of moth-eaten wool blankets strewn across a poor example of a single-man mattress in the center of the room.

He approached the simple iron wood burner, examining the picture-sized door drooping from broken brackets. Opening the door, he blew into the belly of the stove. A puff of jet-black soot blustered back at him as if the burner was angered by being bothered. Silas arranged his bundle of wood inside then dug a half-soaked box of matches from his pack. He struck two matches without yielding a flame before the third stick finally flickered to life. He stood, tossing the match into the stove, and nodded with satisfaction when the wood ignited.

"Well," he exhaled, resting his hands on his hips and spinning in a slow circle, "this is…quaint."

Pursing my lips, I rolled my eyes. "I never promised luxury." I stomped to the stove and threw my stash of wood on the floor at its stubby legs. Flinging my hands up, I added, "I'm not sure what you expected from a run-down shack in the dank belly of a swamp. If you wanted something more lavish, you should have—"

Silas bolted toward me, grabbing my arms to yank me into his chest. Our bodies thumped together.

I harrumphed mid-rant, scowling up at him.

"I don't need luxury. I need you," he whispered. The warmth of his breath swept over my face, caressing the stress-lines from my forehead. His eyes traced the bladed ridge of my nose down to my parted, speechless mouth.

I licked my bottom lip, remembering his bold taste.

He watched my innocent action, and the tender, adoring light in his gaze flared to an impassioned, lustful fire.

His fingers smoothed up my damp sleeves, cresting along my shoulders to skim the length of my collarbones. Skimming his hands down, he grazed the full mounds of my breasts spilling over my corset. Silas glanced at the fifteen or so pearl buttons lining my bodice front and grinned. His thumb and forefinger worked diligently, unlooping each button with a teasing patience.

My heart raced like a herd of cattle being chased by a coyote. Fast, wanton breaths rushed in and out of my lungs, anticipating the glory of his hungry touch exploring every inch of my flesh.

When he bent to gather my dress and drag it up my torso, a tiny whimper of need escaped my throat. Blood pounded in my ears, drowning out the prattling secedes and playful twills of nocturnal birds outside our sanctuary. The war could have started again just outside the door, and I wouldn't have known. All my wits were held hostage by the beautiful man undressing me.

Silas hurled my dress at the foot of the glowing stove. The heat radiating from its gaping mouth rolled over my chilled skin, calling a shutter to quake through me.

Considering I chose comfort over moral fashion when I left his house, I didn't have many undergarments for him to remove. Without taking his eyes from mine, he unhooked the strip of front-clasps keeping my corset closed. Slinging it on the pile to dry with my dress, he slumped to his knees, mouth and eyes round with veneration, like he was praying before a vision of Jesus Christ himself.

"Magnificent," he croaked on a hard swallow.

We had already made love, but he hadn't seen me bare. Somehow, my exposure, and his reaction, spurred the need to hide myself.

Even Edison had not seen me disrobed like this in years. Though, I'd given into the raw need for sexual gratification with Edison, I kept myself from him in this way, always covered by a sheet or a chemise at the very least. It was a protective barrier of sorts.

Now, Silas was peeling away my protective barrier, cracking open my cocoon, and it was unnerving. I was not deserving of such appraisal. Hunching over, I inched my hands up to cover my breasts and hoped he left my petticoat in place.

"No," Silas snapped. He gripped my wrists, easing them back to my sides.

His heavy-lidded eyes perused my breasts with dagger-sharp concentration. He appeared to be memorizing the way they hung like bells and the dusky-rose of my puckered nipples. "Don't you dare," he exhaled on a ragged breath.

I tucked my bottom lip behind my teeth to stifle the protest instinctually settling on my tongue.

He released my arms and hastily wrestled out of his day jacket. He tore his shirt off and unbuttoned his trousers, his focus pinned to my body every second.

I remained static, transfixed by the hard muscles rippling in his shoulders and stomach as he undressed. I admired the thin patch of dark-blonde hair dusting from one small nipple to the other. The two squared slabs of flesh sculpting his strong chest flexed with his eager movements.

His unsteady hands bracketed my wide hips, tugging me toward him. He nuzzled his nose below my navel, burying his face in the soft roundness of my abdomen.

My breath ceased.

I moved my hand to the back of his head but hesitated before touching him.

This was too intimate an act. He shouldn't be digging this deep under my skin. He said he wanted me, no matter what, but if we continued, surely, he'd find something in me that would change his mind.

He rubbed his stubbled chin against my groin, inciting a delicious pain I could feel in my core.

Unable to keep from touching him any longer, I combed my fingers through his shoulder-length waves and squeezed, tipping his head away from my stomach.

He stared up at me, questioningly, his pulsing neck bared to me. The vein beside his throat thrummed at an uncountable rhythm.

He was as vulnerable as I was in this moment.

Fighting my grasp on his hair, he leaned forward. He shimmied the back of my petticoat around to the front, then caught the string between his teeth and pulled the securing bow loose. Grinning, he yanked my underskirt down over my hips, divesting me of the last piece of clothing hiding me from him.

He sucked in a pleased breath, admiring the thatch of dark-red hair veiling my passion-slickened mound. Silas sat back on his heels, his tongue flicking out to wet his lips.

He remained silent so long, I felt the fingers of shame and uncertainty claw at my chest.

My hand twitched with the impulse to conceal my most secret parts. "Silas?" I breathed.

Frenzied eyes darted up to mine, reflecting the stove's fire and his raging desire. He gulped. Resting back on his hands, he maneuvered his legs out from under him then kicked his trousers and drawers off.

Suddenly, my mouth was drier than parchment. His rigid length jutted up to graze his navel. All the moisture in my body gathered between my thighs.

Silas flattened to his back on the dusty floor. He held out his hand, inviting me to join him.

I padded to his side, but he wrapped his fingers around one of my calves, drawing me toward his shoulders. "I want to see you better."

I shook my head.

Ignoring my weak refusal, Silas urged my left foot to raise and land on the opposite side of his body.

Nervous knots tightened in my stomach. Keeping my knees somewhat closed with him lying between my legs, I peered down at the only man to have seen me so completely.

"You have nothing to be ashamed of. You are the most beautiful—the most beguiling—woman I've ever seen. Please…come closer," he beckoned.

I moved to lay next to him, but he locked his hands around my ankles, holding me fast to my spot above him.

Rocking his head side to side. "No, ma'am. Come closer." His stern gaze bore into me like he was trying to cast his thoughts straight into my mind.

"I…I was--"

He interrupted. "Bend down to me, my sweet."

If I bent down, my sex would hover right over his face.

The thrill of indecency and salaciousness heightened my senses, refining the surge of lust swirling in the cabin.

Firm hands scraped up my legs and cupped the backs of my knees. He tugged gently until my legs buckled.

I gasped, tumbling down to land on all-fours above his head. My breath hitched. I looked between my spread thighs, and Silas tilted his head back, grinning at me. He hooked his arms around my upper thighs and hugged me to him.

Closing my eyes, I relaxed into his unforgiving grip on me and relished the feel of his hot breath on my wet folds.

Soft, plushness traced my crease.

I flinched and instantly tried to pull away.

He clamped my thighs around his head, denying me a chance to run. When his slick tongue slipped between my folds once more, I sighed, melting into his mercy without another thought of escaping.

Silas devoured me with his skilled tongue and mouth…suckling…nipping…laving every secreted nerve-ending.

I panted, arching my back and widening my knees to give him all of me. One more flick across my swollen bud, another dip of his tongue into my core, and all my blood pooled into my pelvis.

I throbbed for him.

I quaked for him.

My nipples beaded into aching pebbles. My muscles went rigid. I stilled, no longer rocking my cleft across his mouth. I couldn't swallow or even think. I was so thoroughly wrapped in the silky swath of euphoria, I couldn't move, couldn't produce noise. My pleasured moans hushed, quieted by the enthralling rush of all-encompassing elation that zoomed through my body.

I'd ridden the mountain to the peak, and now, I was tipping over the ledge to the other side.

Silas granted me one more gentle stroke, plummeting me toward the river of satisfaction awaiting just over the crest.

As I gave into the shudders of my climax, he rolled me to the side, laying me on my back. He climbed up my body like a panther claiming his territory, a gleam of possession in his eyes. Hooking one of my knees over his elbow, he folded my leg to my chest and spread me wide open to him.

His plump tip brushed my delicate, wet flesh. He rolled his hips, dragging himself through the slickness he'd created, and smiled.

I tilted my head back, moaning. "Please," I whimpered.

He slid along me, teasing me, rubbing his hardness against my pearl of nerves.

"Please, I need you inside," I begged in a throaty voice.

Silas leaned down, his arms framing my shoulders, caging me in his love. "Tell me you love me, Synthia." He positioned his tip at my opening and barely pushed in, just enough for me taste the fullness he could give. "Tell me you'll be mine forever," he breathed against my ear.

My heart swelled, pounding fervently against my ribs. The last bricks of my wall crumbled and fell away like fine sand.

I cupped his scruffy cheeks in my hands. "I'm yours, my love."

Silas groaned, pleased with my oath, and plunged into me. He lowered his weight onto me, burying himself in my depths.

I stared up at the rusted tin roof, a contented smile pulling at my lips.

Being with Edison, even when we loved each other, never felt like this. My connection with Silas was searing and full of impulsive, explosive energy. We were a lightning storm of temptation and devotion. We were fueled by past sins and future redemption.

I scraped my nails into his tense shoulders, whimpering as he reluctantly dredged himself out of me. When he thrust back in, our moans tangled.

"I love you, Silas."

His breaths blew more rapid on my neck, and he stalled above me. "I love you, Synthia."

Skimming my fingers down the lean ridges of his sides, I urged him to move. "I love you, paramour. Please, don't stop," I whispered on his stubbled jaw.

He pulled out, hefted my leg higher on his arm, then drove deep to my end.

We made love for what felt like many moons, warmed by the iron stove and our affirmation to one another.

Chapter Twenty-Two

An early-morning nip seeped into my bones. I tugged our tattered blanket up to my ears, cursing through chattering teeth. Silas's warm hand drew lazy circles on my spine.

I opened my eyes, too cold to keep sleeping, and pouted at the smoking iron stove. The fire fizzled out in the night, once our sheer exhaustion surpassed our need to keep feeding it.

I reached above my head, testing the pile of fabric rumpled at the stove's legs, and groaned.

"What is it?" Silas asked, kissing my shoulder.

Rolling onto my back, I poked out my bottom lip. "My dress. It's still damp. The fire didn't last long enough to dry it all the way." I craned my neck, kissing him on the lips.

Feathering his fingers over my stomach, he nudged his chin toward the dry leather saddle bags propped against the stove leg. "I have two extra pair of pants in my pack. We'll have to wade back out in our old clothes then change when we get on shore."

Tilting my head back, I looked out the dingy window. The air held a muted azure hue. The sun barely breached the horizon.

My gaze lowered to a small cobalt bottle tipped on its side beneath the window's ledge. A dry cork rested beside it, chewed up by the small animals that dared to gnaw on it. I let my eyes drift from the faded skull and crossbones warning peeling off the bottle of Arsenic to the decaying mouse carcass lying next to the container. It forced me to think of Edison and the poison I dumped in his tea. If there had been enough in Tula's bottle, would I be lying here in Silas's arms right now?

I relaxed my neck and searched Silas's face. "Why did you come here?"

His golden brow pinched at his nose. "I told you, I'd follow you anywhere."

"No, I mean, what brought you to Savannah? What were your goals before you met me?"

His adoring expression sharpened, and he flopped onto his back, cradling his head in his hands. A frustrated breath blew from his perfect mouth. "My mother died from the poor conditions Deveraux required her to work in. The laboring hours with cotton-filled lungs took a harsh toll on her frail body. I worked there, in his factory of slaves, when I was a boy. I'd hoped my hours put in would relieve some of the pressure on my mother. My father died in the war, leaving her to take care of me on her own.

"I came back take over his company, steal every bit of money he's made, and give those workers a chance to live without fearing their lives will end at the mercy of Deveraux's insatiability."

"Take over his company?" I brewed over the thought for a moment, picking apart his actions up until now. "You were going to become a partner…then what?"

"I'd hoped to gain his trust and a valuable position in his business. By his side, I would either stumble across evidence of his abuse and take it to the police, salvaging the pieces afterward," he licked his lips, turning his head to face me, "or, I would kill him and run off with whatever money I could find in his house, which I suspect is a lot. I'd split it among his workers and free them of their obligations to work for him. At least, for a little while."

I laid my head on his chest, committing to memory the persistent thud of his heartbeat. I traced lines up and down the valley defining his abdominal muscles. "You don't want to take a life, Silas. You'll never outrun the guilt. It sticks to you like a shadow."

"How do you know I haven't already?" he whispered.

My fingers stilled. I glanced up at him, waiting for him to explain, but he stayed silent.

We all had our secrets. When he was ready to talk about it, I'd be there to listen without judgement, as he'd done for me.

"We should get going. I want to be there by the time he stuffs his gullet with breakfast." I pushed off the floor and gathered my underclothes.

Silas curled up, propping himself on his elbows to watch me. "What are your plans, she-devil?"

I tied my petticoat in place and fastened my corset. His gaze tracked every move I made unapologetically.

Balling my gown in a tight bundle, I scooted his wrinkled clothes toward him with my foot. "Get dressed." I marched the window and picked up the cobalt bottle, thumbing its cork back in place.

"Synthia?" Silas eyed me nervously, thrusting one leg into his trousers at a time.

"We need to visit Edison's house and procure a couple of his finest cigars."

"I don't think that's a good idea, my sweet," he said, buttoning up his shirt while stuffing his feet into his boots.

"Don't worry, Silas. We are going to get Tula and make a deal Mr. Deveraux hopefully won't refuse." Palming the glass container of dried poisonous residue, I smiled. "If everything goes to plan, you'll get what you came for, I'll get Tula, and she'll get the world."

Chapter Twenty-Three

Climbing the front steps of Mr. Deveraux's home, I glanced behind me. Silas walked tall, his expression a mask of solid confidence and determination. Mr. Thrift stumbled nervously beside him, his gaze flittering between my love and me. He quirked his mouth to the side, uncertain of how our day would end, and held a tight fist around the handle of his satchel. There were papers in there that could change our fate today—all our fates.

Nervous bees flew in my stomach, the sting of worry and dread needle-sharp.

Silas winked at me reassuringly. "Your plan is good. He's a man of self-preservation. Surely, he'll agree. And, if he doesn't..." He patted the gun concealed beneath his sable coat.

I nodded and inhaled, pushing the sleeves of Silas's white shirt up to my elbows. His trousers were loose around my waist, but I'd put on a set of suspenders under his indigo vest to keep them up. With his clothes and my short hair, no one suspected he accompanied a fugitive—the murderous Synthia James—when we traveled through town on our way to Devereux's plantation.

Knock, knock.

I rapped on the front door, noting the expensive craftsmanship of its smooth edges and dense wood. Footsteps scuffled along the floor inside, and a maid yelled out, "I'll get it, sir," in a shrill voice.

Seconds later, she opened his home to us. Her eyes widened when she saw me leaning against the doorjamb, observing her from under the brim of Silas's gambler hat.

I smiled sweetly. "Is the master of the house in, ma'am?"

Her eyes slanted to the room on her left, trepidation paling her rosy cheeks.

Silas stepped forward, pushing her aside. "We'll find him, miss, no need to announce us."

I eased into the foyer behind him, glancing back to make sure Mr. Thrift followed suit.

"Sir," she scoffed, "I can't let you in." She chased after us, her wrinkled hands wringing fistfuls of her dingy apron.

"Seems you already have," I tossed over my shoulder.

Her tiny feet skittered behind us, trying to catch up, but we stayed well in her way, heading off the poor woman's efforts to notify her employer of intruders.

"Mr. Deveraux," Silas greeted, entering the dining room.

Horace's hand froze in front of his face, holding a forkful of eggs inches from his open mouth. His brows drew together in anger at first, then relaxed when he registered who'd interrupted his meal. Closing his empty mouth, he clanged the fork down on his plate, no longer interested in his eggs. Settling back in his high-backed chair, he wiped his hands on a napkin in his lap and flung it onto his plate.

"I tried to stop them, sir," the maid muttered.

Deveraux waved his hand through the air. "Mary, we all know you are shit at answering doors. Go find something useful to do. I can handle our guests from here." A slow smirk spread over his yellowed teeth.

Mary shuffled off, her small whimpers growing farther away as she obeyed her master.

"What can I do for you, Henry?" Deveraux asked, emphasizing the name I'd taken when I was in his house last.

Gritting my teeth to keep my emotions at bay, I side-stepped Silas. "Where is she?"

He traced his thumb along his bottom lip, taking a moment to evaluate my pants, vest, and hat. He was probably deciding my outer attire wasn't a true indication of the strength I held on the inside.

Crossing one long leg over the other, he stared at me and slid his hand down his perfectly groomed beard. It was a gesture I could see him doing, mindlessly, to calm himself when he was nervous or when brooding over an insistent thought that left his brain busy. "The girl is where she belongs."

I rushed toward him, slapping my palms on the table. "She belongs with me, someone who cares about her."

"How do you suppose you'll care for her, Henry? You are a worthless murderer on the run. Do you really think she'll have a better future with you?" He uncrossed his knees and leaned forward, his wicked gaze trying to convince me he had the upper hand. "I give the girl clothes, food, and a roof over her head. She'll learn discipline and respect here…a fine trade for a little servitude, don't you think?"

I lowered my eyes to a piece of imported cheese crumbled on his plate. Doubt was drilling its way back into my spine, and my backbone weakened under his words.

Silas pulled out the chair next to Deveraux and sat. He lifted the revolver from his holster, aiming it at his nemesis with complete composure. "It's really not a matter of whether Miss Tula will be staying with you or not, Horace. The thing that's up for debate is, will Ms. James, Miss Tula, and I be leaving you dead or alive when we go. The decision is up to you."

Deveraux glared down the barrel at Silas. "You can't possibly be serious," he sneered.

Silas rested his elbow on the table. He thumbed the hammer back to engage the bullet aimed at Deveraux. "Dead serious."

The roll of the cylinder made the older man sit a little straighter in his wingback chair.

The sound of china clattering against china came from the doorway. Tula stood a few steps inside the room, holding a tea tray. Her small hands shook, causing the cups and saucers to jangle. Tears spilled down her freckled cheeks, but she kept her lips sewn shut.

I smiled, opening my mouth to tell her how happy I was to see her and that we were leaving this god-forsaken place, but my words fell short when she didn't greet me.

Tula sniffled and carried the tray to the buffet spanning the far wall. She pored tea and scooped sugar into the vessels with her back to me the entire time.

Was she not happy to see me?

Did she decide her home was with her true father?

Swallowing the lump in my throat, I blinked away the wetness gathering in my eyes. I lowered to the chair across from Silas and addressed Deveraux. "I have a proposal."

One shaggy eyebrow perked up on Deveraux's forehead. "A proposal?" He laughed. "What makes you think I'll entertain anything you'll have to offer?"

"Because if you don't, I'll have Mr. Burke pull his trigger and decorate this nice dining room with pieces of your brain. I'm sure your maid will have a time getting the remnants of blood out of your gilded wallpaper, sir."

Silas bent forward, grinning with the revolver wrapped snuggly in his nimble fingers.

The smug smile drained from Deveraux's face when he realized I was serious. He nodded his head once, inviting me to continue.

"I want you to sign your business over to Tula in your will. Assign her sole heir to all your assets with complete control over your affairs. She is your only true heir, anyway, so it shouldn't be hard. Mr. Thrift has drawn up paperwork for this occasion." I nodded to the silent attorney, watching us with timid eyes.

A rolling laugh built in Deveraux's gut and burbled out of his throat with a hint of disbelief. "What in the hell, Henry?" He tilted his head, deciding my sincerity from a different angle. He thought I'd lost my mind for sure. "Absolutely not." He pointed his index finger into the table, bringing emphasis to his next words. "I refuse to give a little half-breed bitch any cent of my company. She deserves no more than my hogs in the pen out back. I've worked too hard to piss it all away at the hands of a woman blacky from a whore mother."

A sharp gasp sounded behind me. The tension in the room stirred when Tula spun around to face Deveraux. She was seething, her cheeks reddening as she shot imaginary daggers at her father. Without a word, she took three stiff strides across the room and set a steaming cup of tea in front of Deveraux. Her slender hand lingered on the handle while she bore her hate down on him.

He ignored her, staying fixated on me. "What would I get in return?"

"We'll leave here today, with Tula, and never bother you again."

He moved to stand. Silas waggled the gun at Deveraux's head, clicking his tongue in warning. Deveraux froze, weighing the degree of threat, then lowered back into his seat.

He gnawed on the inside of his right cheek for a moment, mulling over my proposal. His life for Tula and his empire after death.

His calculating gaze drifted to the young woman at his side. He narrowed his eyes.

"And if I don't, you'll kill me?"

I leaned my hip into the table and crossed my arms. "If you don't let Tula leave here with us, yes. She goes no matter what.

"As for the business arrangement…if you don't sign the papers, I will leak every filthy secret you've buried over the past twenty years to all your partners and their partners until your company flounders belly-up. We'll see how much they like working with the likes of a murderer and rapist."

"You don't have any proof," he growled.

"I have detailed accounts of all the dirt Edison found out about you and the sources he used to acquire this information. Those who are still willing to work with you after we tell your sins? Well, let's just say, I have no problem bringing justice into my own hands. I hear it's a little easier to bleed a pig once you've stomached it for the first time."

He looked at me with such intensity, my skin prickled. Inside, I wanted to fold into a ball and hide from him, to give into his power and admit defeat.

I glanced at Tula. She rocked listlessly from one foot to the other behind Deveraux's chair. Her hands were balled over her heart and silent tears trailed down her round cheeks.

She was the reason I was here. I couldn't forget that. She was my world, and I would not leave this house without her.

My gaze darted to Silas. He sat in his seat, shoulders pulled back. He was here to finish what he started so long ago. He was here for me. Cool, steady confidence radiated off his skin and reached out to me, giving me the shred of determination I needed to stand my ground.

Deveraux swiped his hand over his mouth then down his beard. "So, it's my life for this worthless girl, and my company now for the title of all I have after my death?

I nodded, giving him a chance to weigh his heavy choices for a few seconds longer.

"Thrift," he barked, "the papers?"

Mr. Thrift opened his mouth to say something but stopped when I shot him a warning glance. He fumbled with the brass latch on his satchel then retrieved the newly penned will from its dark depths.

Tula rushed out the door, returning moments later with a pen and inkwell. She clanked the glass container down on the table and slid it within Deveraux's reach.

He held the will between his finger and thumb, skimming over the words with carful diligence. His gaze flicked to each one of us then back at the parchment. "I guess it won't matter much what happens once I'm dead, will it? I have no other children and Petunia died a decade ago." He picked up the pen, hovering it over the onyx liquid. "The girl's not worth the fuss, anyway."

His right hand dipped the nib in black ink and scrolled his signature along the bottom of the paper.

He flung the pen across the table as if it were a dangerous weapon then threw the papers at Mr. Thrift.

We did it.

We would walk out of here with everything we wanted—Tula, her rights to his company, a future for the people he'd hurt for so many years—now, all we had to do was wait for him to die.

It was a small thing in the grand scheme of our future.

No one could predict their death, right?

If we were lucky, he'd keel over the moment we stepped outside the door. One could only hope.

"Cigar, Mr. Deveraux?" I plucked two fat rolls of tobacco, freshly clipped, from my shirt pocket. One was banded with a gold label, and one was banded in red. "A smoke of peace between businessmen." I twirled the red-labeled cigar between my thumb and finger.

Red for blood.

Red for revenge.

He rolled his eyes but held out his hand, a glutton for indulgences, and accepted the cigar I fondled.

Silas placed his gun back into his holster before pulling a box of matches from his shirt pocket. He struck a match and cupped his hand around the flame until Deveraux sucked on his cigar enough times to set the cherry on fire.

I leaned over the table, sucking on my own cigar until it was lit by Silas's flame. Our gazes locked over the flickering light. Promises of a shared victory and dreams danced in our eyes.

After a few more puffs, I pinched the end of my cigar and offered it to Silas.

He stood, taking the smoke, and gestured toward the door. "Shall we, ladies?"

I smiled. "Mr. Deveraux, I'm glad we could come to an agreement. Mr. Thrift will notify us when it is our turn to assume responsibility of your earnings. And, please refrain from making any changes to the will once we leave...it would be bad for your health." I grinned, knowing he understood the dark meaning behind my words. I tipped my hat toward him. "I wish you an abundance of happiness for the rest of your life, sir."

He didn't bother standing to see us out. Instead, he gulped down the contents of his teacup and inhaled another deep tug from the cigar I gave him.

The three of us walked out of the room, across the foyer, and through the doorway, holding our heads high.

Chapter Twenty-Four

Standing at the murky water's edge with my toes curling in the muck, I pulled my shawl tighter around my shoulders. The wind was biting this morning, but I didn't know how many days I had left to visit my favorite spot.

Silas and I retired to bed soon after Tula last night, once our nerves calmed from our encounter with Mr. Deveraux. The days seemed painfully long and tortuous over the past week, and we all clung to the security of Silas's home, knowing our time there would likely be short. We slept soundly, our exhaustion too overwhelming to converse and make plans. However, we suspected Sheriff Cunningham would hunt for us soon, considering the escape Silas and I made the day before.

Tangerine rays of the dawn's sun pierced through the Mangroves reaching up from the swamp floor. I stared at the blades of light, letting my vision blur in thought. I calculated the chance of Horace's quick death, wondering if he was strong enough to evade the oily fingers of his reaper.

Lowering my gaze to my feet, I honed my thoughts to the tasks I'd have to accomplish today: collecting more clothes, packing the horses and wagons, and devising a track across the country that would keep us better hidden than our last attempts to leave Savannah.

A shaft of sunlight lazily swept over my mud-caked toes. Something silver poked out of the dirt next to my heel and shone under the wavering beam.

Narrowing my eyes, I bent to examine the reflective object. My fingers trembled, detecting a familiarity I was afraid to admit. I reached out and clawed it from the swamp's clutches. I rose, flipping the small, silver disk in my hand, smudging away the layer of soil clumped on its surface.

A gasp stuck in my throat. It was a pocket watch. Not just any pocket watch—Edison's. My wide eyes flittered over the watery dregs of his land. He never came out here; it was why I took my own solace in this place.

In the distance, an alligator waggled off an embankment, yawning his long snout open before slamming his powerful jowls shut.

A shutter snaked up my back. The suspicion that this was Edison's last resting place hit me hard, like a hammer driving me—the final nail—into his coffin.

Callused fingers skimmed up my arms, and warm breath grazed my bare neck. "I didn't mean for it to happen this way," Silas whispered against my ear.

I craned my neck back to look at him. Sorrow and regret swam in the pools of his slate eyes. I could see, without a doubt, he was not a malicious man. Whatever happened here, it wasn't because Silas's heart was cold like mine. Yes, he was willing to kill for me. If pushed hard enough, he would do whatever it took to keep Tula and me safe, but he didn't have it in him to murder somebody in cold blood.

For now, I trusted the quarrel he and Edison had ended the only way it could, and with little blame resting on Silas's shoulders.

His lips parted. He inhaled deeply, his chest rising around his confession.

I pressed my finger onto his lips, hushing him. I was not his priest. I did not need him to surrender his guilts or explain the actions he took to deal with an uncompromising, wicked man.

Stretching up onto my toe tips, I removed my finger and replaced it with my mouth. We kissed, dissolving any shred of uncertainty he might have about my feelings.

He pulled away, resting his forehead against mine. "Sheriff Cunningham is waiting for us at the house."

A rock of dread sank in my stomach. This was it. We had less time than I'd hoped. "They came for me so soon," I whimpered, clutching his shirt in my fists.

"We could run. We could take off now, see how far we could get."

I shook my head frantically. "Tula. She'll go back to that horrible man." I released his shirt and wiped the tears spilling down my cheeks with the heel of my palm. "If I go, if I turn myself in now, perhaps they will let her stay with you. Cunningham has his suspicions about Deveraux. Perhaps, they'll forgive you for harboring a fugitive and take pity on her. You and Tula can have a life without looking over your shoulder every second."

An objection was building behind Silas's forlorn expression. I tore away from him and marched toward the Burke house.

He jogged beside me, latching onto my upper arm. "This is crazy, Synthia."

I paused, pulling away from his grip gently. "What's crazy is the idea of us getting away with everything we've done without a single consequence. It's crazy to think a murderess and a young mixed girl can find peace with a good man like you, while judgmental, bigoted, powerful heathens loom over us, eager to tear us down. There has to come a point when we stop trying to revive a dead horse and accept the situation."

Silas's shoulders fell, knowing what I spoke was true.

We walked in silence back to his home, our hands linked together. His house even seemed sad for me. Its windows appeared dark and dreary, its long, shallow porch drooped slightly at the end posts in a stiff frown.

Mr. Cunningham swung the front door open and strolled out, shadowed by the porch's overhang. He stopped at the top of the steps, perching his fists on his hips. waiting for us to come to him. Schooling his expression into a mask of indifference, he avoided giving any prelude to his reason for visiting.

Silas and I slowed at the worn footpath stretching out from under the bottom step.

I glanced to each side of the house, worried his ruthless bounties would spring around the corners in an ambush.

"I'm alone, Ms. James," Cunningham assured.

An orange flare of sun cresting Silas's roof forced me to squint up at the sheriff. "You're so sure I'll go easy?"

He took each step at an easy pace, lowering himself to my level. "Should I have a reason to think otherwise?" His bushy, graying brow crooked up.

I peered down at the dusting of red soil dried on his tan boots and shook my head. "No, sir."

I encircled my right hand around my left wrist, messaging the tender skin there. Cunningham was going to slap the shackles on me at any minute now.

"Did you pay Mr. Deveraux a visit yesterday, Ms. James?"

I glanced at Silas for a beat. Crossing my arms over my stomach, I nodded. "Yes. We had some affairs to finalize. Managed to work it all out without making trouble, though."

Cunningham's mouth twitched at one corner. "Is that right?"

"For the love of Saint Julian." Silas grated beside me. "I gave you evidence showing she was only acting under Edison's manipulation. We didn't harm Mr. Deveraux, so why are you really here? Are you still going to arrest her, knowing what torment Edison put her through?"

The sheriff cleared his throat, slitting his eyes at Silas's outburst in a pointed warning.

Silas raked his fingers through his fair hair and paced in a tight circle behind me. The tension of his need to keep me protected, without actually being able to, flared off him like a blazing pyre.

Cunningham's gaze slid to me. "Ms. James, I'm here today because of the affairs you tended to with Deveraux. I was informed you negotiated some changes in his will. It would be remiss of me to not investigate at least the tiniest bit before the actions of said will were carried out.

"Apparently, sometime after you left, Deveraux's maid entered his dining room to check on the miserable man. She said he was in quite a mood that morning, and, with your arrival, she knew he would be next to intolerable. Ms. Janie states Mr. Deveraux often partook in calming his stress with an opium pellet, chased by a splash of whiskey. Ms. Janie served his concoction as usual. However, to her surprise, this time was different. Within a half hour, Horace Deveraux was found lying, belly up, on his extravagantly carpeted floor."

The sheriff clasped his hands behind his back, lifting his chin to the sky. "Now, I feel certain a man who does this type of ritual regularly can handle a pellet of opium without dying in most circumstances." His observant eyes darted to meet mine. He blew out an audible breath of frustration. "Stranger things have happened, though." He pressed his lips together, tapping his forefinger against them in thought then asked, "Would you have any idea why I might find a half-burned cigar containing high-quality tobacco and a dusting of strange white powder?"

Biting my lower lip, I peeked back at Silas's frozen form. He'd stop pacing the second the sheriff mentioned my added substance.

We both knew Cunningham would have had to cut the cigar open to find it.

"I only ask because I questioned Mr. Thrift, and he noted you gave him a cigar as a peacemaker after your deal."

Lucky for Mr. Thrift, he'd not given the sheriff any details about my barter with him. He was easy enough to pay off in exchange for drawing the new will and witnessing the finalization. The man said he never liked Deveraux anyway. With the amount we agreed to give him, I felt positive he'd keep our pact until his own death.

I shrugged a shoulder. "I'm not sure what you're referring to, sir. The cigar came from Edison's best stash. I don't know why anybody would add anything other than tobacco in there."

Cunningham smirked, bobbing his head. "I thought that might be the case." He paused, rolling around another thought in his head. "And the bitter tea Miss Tula served him?"

I wanted to shake my head, contesting her involvement in Mr. Deveraux's passing, but I cemented my features in place and looked on with feigned ignorance. If I reacted too strongly, it would only suggest our guilt. "I'm sorry, Sheriff, I had little time to observe Tula during my conversation with Mr. Deveraux, but it is doubtful she did anything ill-natured. She is just a young girl, a bird in a cage. There's not a malicious bone in her body."

A cool breeze swirled around us, and Sheriff Cunningham flipped his jacket collar up to shield his neck. Snickering, he said, "That, my dear, is what's doubtful." He pulled out folded parchment from a hidden pocket under his jacket. Eyeing Silas, he stretched his hand out to me. "I suppose these are yours now."

I pinched my brows together, hesitant to take the papers he presented. "What are they?"

"A better future, I hope, Ms. James." He smiled, the gesture void of any suspicion he implied before. "Considering I cannot determine what killed Horace—be it the cigar, the tea, or the sedative Ms. Janie delivered to him—I've come to an impasse. For all I know, it was all three of you, and none are truly at fault, your actions merely feeding one another's. Because of the lack of evidence in the ridiculously obvious evidence, I cannot bring myself to arrest any one of you in good conscience."

I fumbled with the papers, unfolding them as I processed what the sheriff admitted. Silas moved closer, hovering over my shoulder. Tears welled my eyes when I scanned over the first page. It was Deveraux's will.

"Mr. Thrift confirmed everything was the way it should be. Tula is now the sole owner of Deveraux's fortune. I trust you'll help her keep his estate and business in good running order until she is old enough to handle it herself?"

I nodded emphatically, shuffling to the next paper.

"And that is Tula's slave paper. No one should have it but Tula," he said in a stern tone.

I sniffled, drying the deluge of tears streaming down my face with my shawl. "Does this mean... you're not going to arrest me?"

He cupped his hand over my upper arm, ducking his head down to look me in the eyes. "Mr. Pike's journal was enough to convince the judge to rethink your sentence. Despite the money piling in his pockets from those wanting to dispose of you, this town might think twice about keeping him in his position should he lynch a young woman for doing something she was forced into."

Silas exhaled in relief. His warm hand slipped around my waist, drawing me closer to him.

Cunningham noted Silas's subtle movements and grinned. He touched a finger to his hat, dipping his head once in salutation. "You take care of Miss Tula... and each other."

The man who I thought would deliver me to my death skirted around us, strolling to the horse eating apples from Silas's apple tree at the edge of the yard.

He pardoned me.

I buckled into Silas's chest, hiding my face in my hands. The weight of my demise floated off my shoulders like a plume.

"Oh," the thuds of Cunningham's boots hitting the dry ground halted, "speaking of Mr. Pike..."

My body tensed, and I jerked my head up to look at the sheriff.

"In case you were wondering, he seems to have packed his belongings and fled Savannah. No one has heard a peep from him. Should he return, please let me know, and I'll—"

"He'll not be bothering us anymore," Silas interjected.

"Sure," the wise sheriff agreed. A silent exchange of understanding passed between the two from yards away.

Cunningham tapped the brim of his hat once again then collected his horse and left.

Prologue

I stabbed my trowel into the loose soil one last time. Tossing the small brown seed into the hole, I smiled and scanned over the lush rows of purplish-blue flowers swaying in the summer wind. It was turning out to be a good season for our Indigo crops.

A long shadow cut into my view, followed by a shovel piercing into the soft ground next to me.

Shielding my eyes with my hand, I squinted up at Silas. His tanned chest glistened with droplets of salty sweat brought on by working the fields all day.

I smiled then finished scooping dirt back into the hole. Hopefully, the seed nestled under the soil would mature into a robust hybrid shrub we could sell for a pretty penny.

We worked on this particular combination of species for a year, creating something in such high demand we could barely keep up with orders. Silas recruited Mr. Adams as a partner, providing the cotton we dyed and sold to clothing manufacturers.

Together, our business flourished. Deveraux's partners fell in line, too afraid to lose their shirts, and their freedom from jail, if they didn't comply. They discovered Silas and I running things made their lives much more agreeable.

"Did you see her?" I asked, resting back on my heels.

He dropped to the ground and draped his elbows on his knees. "Yes. She came home about an hour ago." He threaded a stem of our flowers through his fingers, gently letting the small indigo blooms skip across his skin.

"Good. I hate when she stays in town. I feel like there's a piece of us missing."

My love grinned and bumped his shoulder into mine. "She's a responsible young woman who can take care of herself now, Synthia."

I poked my lip out, pouting. Time had sifted away from us so fast. "Don't remind me," I groaned.

"That beau of hers was seen perusing the diamond selection at Theodora's Jewelry yesterday." He chuckled. "Hattie even saw him stealing a rather passionate kiss from her on their stroll after dinner the other night."

My eyes widened, and I slapped his arm. "Don't say such things."

Silas winced playfully. "Edwin's a good man. He'll make her an honest woman."

Nodding, I leaned into his side and picked a tiny leaf trapped in his dusting of chest hair. "I know. I just don't want to accept she is a grown woman with suiters. I'd love to keep her my little girl until she's thirty."

Tula soaked up every drop of knowledge that trickled into her vicinity after we told her of Deveraux's death. The girl was determined to better herself and reverse as much of Deveraux's damage as she could. She learned the business of managing a cotton factory from the workers who stayed on when we took over. Then, she turned the cotton factory into an indigo distillery with Edwin Charlemagne's help.

Now, Tula spent her days overseeing her very loyal workers and making sure her inheritance continued to make money for her, as well as every soul operating the machines of her legacy. In doing this, she not only changed her destiny, she fulfilled Silas's promises to his mother.

Silas swatted me with the stem of dainty flowers, then peered at the peach and gold hues lingering on the horizon. "She's nineteen. It's time for our girl to soar."

Soon, the field would come alive with hundreds of twinkling lights, turning our long day's labor into a playground for fireflies. Tula, Silas, and I made many happy memories over the course of our years together, and I wished on each firefly for more to bless our future.

"Let's go in before the mosquitos start biting. Hattie has potato soup waiting for us." Silas rose, coaxing me up with a gentle tug on my arm.

I brushed the dirt off my skirt then took his hand, following him to our home.

We'd chosen to stay in Silas's house, since Savannah didn't hold any more dangers over our heads. This city was where we fought the hardest battles of our lives. It would've been a shame to leave when it wasn't necessary any longer, especially after sacrificing so much of ourselves here.

I glanced to the east, deciding to skip my late evening walk in the woods. Spending the night wrapped in Silas's arms was much more enticing. Through a small separation in the trees, I caught a glimpse of

Edison's sagging roof. His house sat empty and lifeless on the other side of those trees, some distance away, rotting, year after year.

Once in a while, I found myself wandering into his yard, staring at the decaying structure, praying the terrible moments from my past decayed within its walls. Usually, I just kept my distance and pitied the person I was when I lived there.

As Silas, Tula, and I rebuilt our lives, forever linked by love, I gladly eased into the woman I was today. I was not proud of my past deeds, but I was proud of where they led me.

We did not speak of the cigar I willingly gave Horace Deveraux after Cunningham's visit four years ago. Nor did we speak of the tea Tula prepared with her back turned to us. I didn't see her slip the laudanum into his drink, but I knew it was her.

It was not important who carried the blame for his death. We all shouldered it, without regret.

Silas's part in Edison's disappearance did not matter either.

It only mattered that we were together, forever bound by our love. We were safe from those who made us all guilty sinners.

And our revenge was so sweet.

About Haven Cage

Haven Cage lives in the Carolinas with her husband and son. After many years of dabbling with drawing, painting, and working night shift in the medical field, she decided to try her hand at writing.

Unfortunately, her love for books came later in life and proved to add a healthy challenge during her writing journey. Determined to hone her craft, though, she soaks up as much information as she can, spends her free time tapping away in her favorite local coffee shop, and keeps a good book in hand whenever possible.

What began as a hobby has grown into a way of escape and the yearning to take her journey farther, her love for writing and reading deepening along the way.

Haven loves to socialize and hear from her fans. Connect with her at the following links:

Facebook.com/HavenCage/

Twitter: @HavenCage

Instagram: @Haven Cage

Pinterest: Haven Cage

Look for Haven on Goodreads.com, and add her to your bookshelf!

Visit her site at www.authorhavencage.com, and sign up for her newsletter to get updates sooner, receive exclusive promotional deals, and play Haven's Puzzlers for chances to win book prizes!

If you enjoyed this book, please leave a review as it is how authors succeed in the publishing world. Without the reader's love, we would be nowhere.

Thanks for your interest and support!

Books by Haven Cage

The Faltering Souls Series

Nevaeh Richards thinks she has found a chance to leave her homeless life behind. When the spirit of the only father she knows is wrongfully taken to Hell, Nevaeh is hurled into a world haunted by monstrous demons, rogue Guardian angels, love that is beyond her control, and a soul-threatening choice between the inherent evil inside her and the faltering faith she is struggling to grasp.

Nevaeh has to face the overpowering gravity of her choice to save those she loves while striving for strength to fight her greatest threat—herself.

Trial after trial, Nevaeh's loved ones have struggled to save her from a dark destiny. The time has finally come for her to return home and join the Earth-bound angels in a war threatening to destroy the Human race. Is it really Nev who's walking the Earthly plane, though?

The Perilously Pretty Series

Vivienne may play the role of a quiet, docile nightclub singer and waitress for her friends and family, but, behind closed doors, she gives into an insatiable hunger no man can escape.

Penniless and jaded governess, Synthia James, is trapped with her employer, a man she once loved but now despises. His obsession with money and stature has corrupted them both. When he bids their young housemaid to kill a man who threatens his business, Synthia's maternal instincts take over, and she commits the heinous deed herself.